# Waiting for Peace

Helen,

May God give you grace and peace.

Rhonda Sanders

Is. 43:2

# RHONDA SANDERS

TATE PUBLISHING
AND ENTERPRISES, LLC

Published by Tate Publishing & Enterprises, LLC
127 E. Trade Center Terrace | Mustang, Oklahoma 73064 USA
1.888.361.9473 | www.tatepublishing.com

Tate Publishing is committed to excellence in the publishing industry. The company reflects the philosophy established by the founders, based on Psalm 68:11,
*"The Lord gave the word and great was the company of those who published it."*

Book design copyright © 2014 by Tate Publishing, LLC. All rights reserved.
*Cover design by Rodrigo Adolfo*
*Interior design by Jomel Pepito*

Published in the United States of America

ISBN: 978-1-62854-111-3
Fiction / General
14.03.13

# Dedication

*Waiting for Peace* is dedicated to the woman, who has been my biggest supporter. She has been my reality check when I was wandering aimlessly, my rock of strength when I was too weak on my own, my voice of wisdom when I thought I knew everything, my foundation when I lost my footing, my friend when I have needed one most. She believed in me when I had given up on myself, and she has demonstrated the depth of true unconditional love. I love you, Mama.

# Introduction

Feeling forsaken by the man she counted on the most, Janet's confidence in God's promises is shaken. Burdened by the pain of lost hopes, she must struggle to revive both her faith and her marriage, searching for a way to pick up the pieces of her shattered dreams and pull herself together. Yet, until Janet learns to accept the things she cannot change and to depend on the Lord, trusting in his plan and his timing, she will always be waiting for peace because true peace comes only from God.

# Prologue

"Is this seat taken?" a deep voice asked hopefully, his three-piece suit straight out of a magazine, collar unbuttoned and burgundy tie loosened. She took another sip of wine, averting her eyes to the food on her plate.

"I'm waiting on someone," Janet replied, not daring to meet the gaze of the man standing by her table so close she could smell the faint musky aroma of his aftershave.

"My apologies," the stranger replied regretfully. "Enjoy your evening." As the gentleman walked away, Janet twirled the white gold ring on her left hand, feeling lonelier now than before.

She hadn't told him a total lie. She *was* waiting for someone, but he was on a plane headed out of the country and essentially out of her life, possibly for good. What was it he had said nonchalantly before kissing her on the forehead and boarding the plane? Janet squinted in thought.

*This long break will give us both the time we need to think.* Not *I love you so much* or *I'm going to miss you every day.*

Nope.

Not her husband. His last words to her were that they needed time apart to think.

Janet flagged the waiter down for a refill. Tonight, thinking was the last thing she wanted to do. Thinking hurt too much.

Nine months and sixteen days until her date would finally arrive home from his international business trip and twenty-hour flight from the damned sandbox, his three-piece suit finished off not with polished oxfords but rather with combat boots.

And when he finally did walk back through their front door, Janet wasn't sure if she would still be there waiting for him.

Or if he would even care.

*Chapter 1*

Janet focused her gaze on the peeling corner of the wallpaper behind her doctor's head, blinking determinedly to force her eyes to stay dry. Her blank stare failed to conceal her building disappointment with each word spoken by the man in the white coat.

"I don't think it is in your best interests to continue with these treatments right now," he said with concern. Dr. Gunner scanned her chart in his hands. Then the gray-haired man wheeled his little stool over to the exam table where the thirty-year old woman sat cross-legged bouncing her foot back and forth nervously.

"I know this isn't what you want to hear right now, but I believe you should put your plans of starting a family on hold for a while and focus on yourself and your own health." As he continued to explain how her blood pressure had reached pre-hypertensive levels, likely due to her mounting stress and the high dosage of hormones she had been taking, Janet only half listened.

She focused hard on the pastel wallpaper. *They should really update this office,* she thought, distracting herself from the key matter at hand.

"Janet?"

"Oh, I'm sorry." She shook her head. "What did you ask me?"

"I asked how you would feel about going back on birth control for a while," Dr. Gunner repeated cautiously as though not to upset her. "I…"

Janet's gaze dropped to her lap as she answered quietly, "You know I really don't want to do that."

"Well, hun, I think this is something you and Marcus need to talk about."

He paused, carefully analyzing her downcast face. "Janet, you've been taking these hormones for so long that I'm concerned your body is becoming overwhelmed. I know we've talked about this before when you had the laparoscopy surgery several years ago, but conceiving is often difficult for women with endometriosis. It may be time to step back and let your body rest and get back to normal."

*Normal,* she thought. *What would that feel like?*

As she thanked the doctor and told him she would consider his suggestion, Janet contemplated how to tell her husband. The longer the conception process had dragged on, the more distant he had become, and she was afraid of how this new development might impact their already-strained relationship.

She paid her co-pay at the front desk, then walked out the double doors toward her car across the parking lot.

After tossing her purse into the passenger seat, Janet turned the key in the ignition. Her eyelids drooped as she inhaled deeply through her nose and leaned back against the headrest.

"Why is everything so difficult?" she exhaled in a whisper.

A single tear dropped onto the side of her cheek and slowly trickled down to her chin before she brushed it away with the back of her hand. The pit of her stomach ached with emotions she couldn't ignore.

Disappointment.

Fear.

Need.

Worry.

Some days, she dragged these feelings around everywhere she went, but today the roles seemed reversed. Janet felt as though they were dragging her.

Especially the worry. *What is he going to say? What if he decides it's not worth it? What if he has had enough and wants to give up? What if...* the questions circled like a Ferris wheel in Janet's mind.

In her heart, Janet feared the wheel would soon stop, leaving her stuck in a bucket at the top and peering at the empty fairgrounds below.

By the time Janet had arrived home, her anxiety levels were high and her heartbeat erratic. She had spent the drive home trying to decide the best way to initiate the inevitable discussion she and Marcus needed to have.

Janet checked on the roast in the crock pot as soon as she got home. The meat shredded just like it was supposed to when she stuck it with a fork, so she switched the slow cooker to warm and grabbed an apron from the pantry.

She took the corn meal out of the freezer and began to mix up a batch of cornbread. With the mixture poured into a cast iron pan and stuck in the oven on 375 degrees, Janet began dipping out several ladles full of juice into a small mixing bowl. Then, she whisked in a packet of brown gravy mix before returning it to the slow cooker.

A can of green beans made a quick side dish as Janet poured them over into a small pot. She then searched through the refrigerator for some fresh carrots to steam as well. All the while, the conversation she needed to pose over dinner racked her thoughts.

"We need to talk," she practiced the conversation starter aloud. Janet shook her head thinking she sounded too grave. She ran some warm water over the baby carrots, filling the pot half way to the rim.

"Can we talk about something for a bit?" she asked with a tentative smile. Nope. He might just say no if she phrased it that way.

"There's something I need to tell you" sounded too suspicious, like she'd been hiding a dead body in the basement for the last ten years. She sat the pot on the stove and turned the eye on high before wiping her hands with a clean dishtowel.

She peaked through the oven glass at the cornbread, which was fluffing up nicely, and made sure the cook timer was set. In the kitchen, that timer was her best friend. If she forgot to set it, she'd end up with inedible corn briquettes.

After untying the apron strings from around her waist, she laid the apron on the counter by the stove. She turned the fan over the stove on low before walking down the hall to the bedroom to freshen up before Marcus arrived home from work.

He would be ready for supper, and she needed to be ready for him.

The talk they needed to have wouldn't be an easy one, especially considering how seldom they spoke to each other lately. Most of their conversations seemed forced, and this one would be much more complicated than deciding who would pick up milk at the grocery store after work.

She kicked her flats into the closet, hung her belt on a hook on the back of the door, and bent over to touch her toes.

"Ughhh…" she moaned as she held the stretch, gripping the back of her calves and tucking her chin. "I need to join a gym."

As she slowly rolled her body back to a standing position, Janet shuffled her fingers through her hair then tucked the strands behind her ears. The nervous tightness in her chest pained when she took a deep breath, and she forced the air back out with a groan.

Just as she returned to the kitchen and was tying on her apron, Janet heard the rumble of Marcus's car pulling into the driveway. The car door slammed, and the empty pit in her stomach came back with a jolt.

*God, please don't let him get mad,* she prayed silently while she stirred the green beans. She turned off the stove and moved the pots to trivets to cool a bit while she set the table.

Marcus came into the kitchen and began emptying the pockets of his khakis as he did every day after work. Keys placed neatly on their hook on the wall, coins and chapstick in the ceramic bowl, and wallet on the counter.

"I'm starving," he said, exactly as she had known he would.

The kitchen seemed smaller when he walked into it. His tall, slender frame dominated the space as he began unbuttoning the sleeves of his dress shirt while walking toward the refrigerator.

"It's almost ready," Janet said. "I'm setting the table now."

Marcus pulled the sweet tea out of the refrigerator and poured himself a glass, using up the last in the pitcher. "Did you make more tea?" he asked as he sat the empty pitcher down on the counter by the fridge.

"I didn't realize we were almost out, sorry," she apologized as she moved the last of the food to the table.

Marcus sat down on one side of the built-in banquette and began fixing his plate while Janet fixed herself a glass of water and put the empty tea pitcher in the sink.

She slid into the other side of the banquette and began to fill her plate with roast and vegetables. Tense silence hung in the air as they both began to eat.

*What should I say?* Janet asked herself, still trying to figure out how best to broach the subject.

"I went to the doctor today," she eased into the topic.

Marcus continued to eat his roast as though Janet had not spoken.

*This may be even harder than I thought.* Janet cleared her throat. If subtly easing into the conversation didn't work, she might as well dive on in headfirst.

"Dr. Gunner suggested I go back on birth control for a little while." *That should get his attention.*

"Hmm," Marcus responded chewing purposefully. Janet waited for a reaction as he slowly stabbed his green beans with the fork.

Nothing.

*Hmmmm!* she wanted to scream. The doctor was concerned about her health and advised her to stop trying to have a baby, something they had both wanted for a long time, and all Marcus could say was *hmmm*?

"Okay," he added before plopping another bite of roast into his mouth. He chewed for a moment, then reached for his glass and downed the last few drops. "Is there anything else to drink since the tea is gone?"

Janet swallowed hard and told him there were probably some can drinks in the fridge. He drank the last of the tea in his glass, but didn't get up from the table.

Staring at his empty glass, Janet knew he expected her to get up and fix the drink for him. Usually she would have, but something about his nonchalant attitude made her stay seated. After the waves of emotions she'd been riding all afternoon, all he could say was *Hmmm, okay.*

But it wasn't okay. *She* wasn't okay. Did he not understand that?

"Dr. Gunner says my blood pressure has gotten too high, and he thinks my body needs a break from all the hormones," she explained as she toyed with the beans and carrots on her plate.

"We all need a break from your hormones," he joked under his breath.

She didn't laugh.

"Seriously? I'm trying to talk to you about something important, and you're making jokes!" Janet exclaimed softly. The words came out slowly as she struggled to control her building irritation.

"There's those hormones rearing their ugly heads," Marcus couldn't help himself. When he saw an opportunity for a joke at her expense, he always seemed to take it. Sometimes she needed the laugh. Then again, sometimes he took it too far, like right now.

Janet's face started to turn red.

*Does he not see that I'm upset?* Janet wondered as she rose from the table to begin loading the dishwasher. *Or does he not care?*

Either way, his lack of concern for her or about the situation hurt.

"I want to know your opinion. If I go back on birth control, then we're putting off trying to have a baby. Is that what you want?"

Marcus started to rise from the table. "Well, if you stop going to the doctor so much, that would sure save us a lot of money. Plus," he paused to shrug his shoulders, "I've about decided that I don't want kids anyway."

Janet looked at him in disbelief.

"You've decided what?"

"I don't think I want kids," he repeated.

Janet felt her heartbeat freeze, and she understood what people meant when they said their life flashed before their eyes.

"What has brought this on? Where is this coming from?" she squeaked with panic in her voice.

"I've just been thinking about it. They're too expensive and a lot of trouble." He popped open a can he had retrieved from the refrigerator and stood in front of the door. "A baby is already costing me a fortune, and you aren't even pregnant yet."

Marcus motioned to the bills on the counter and muttered, "Too bad we didn't get a bailout." He walked into the living room, and she heard the recliner squeak as he propped his feet up.

She quietly put the last of the leftovers in the refrigerator, then put a tab in the slot on the dishwasher door and turned the cycle on normal wash.

*Now what?* She thought to herself, standing in the clean kitchen with her hands on her hips. Was she supposed to go sit in the living room and watch television with him like everything was okay?

Deciding to take a shower and go to bed instead, Janet headed down the hall to the master suite. Normally she would take a hot shower, but tonight she opted for crisp cold water to bring her out of her state of shock.

*He doesn't think he wants kids,* she thought over and over as the water poured over her body, the depleted body she'd been pumping full or hormones and prenatal vitamins, the body she'd indulged in the occasional cheesecake because a few extra pounds wouldn't matter since she hoped to soon become pregnant.

*He doesn't think he wants kids.*

*He doesn't think he wants kids.*

She dried off and went to bed, pulling the comforter up tightly around her even though the summer heat only required a thin sheet. Out of habit, she picked up the magazine on her nightstand and flipped it open like she did every night.

Janet didn't want to cry as she flipped through pages. *Surely he didn't mean it,* she told herself.

But she wasn't convinced.

The parenting magazine she'd been subscribing to for months only made her heart ache more, so she laid it back on the nightstand face down. Was she supposed to cancel her subscription now? Janet was so confused.

And shocked. It was so out of the blue. But then again, subconsciously she had worried this might happen because conceiving was taking so long. Part of her had thought all along that she needed to rush things before he changed his mind. She had thought that was a silly notion before.

"Guess not," she muttered.

The next morning, Janet slipped out of bed early as she did most Saturdays. As she slid on her pink slippers and quietly tip-toed down the hall toward the kitchen, she wondered how people slept so late on the weekends. She certainly couldn't. Her body awoke like clockwork as though Saturday were another work day.

While a pot of coffee brewed, Janet gathered up the stack of mail she put off every week until Saturday morning and stacked the pile neatly on the kitchen table along with her checkbook, envelopes, and stamps. Sticking with her usual routine gave Janet a sense of normalcy despite the turmoil she felt inside.

*What are we going to do?* she kept thinking. She had to convince him that he didn't really want to give up. Maybe the answer was to stop trying to have a baby for a while to give her body and his mind some rest from the stress, but how would that affect their relationship if they did? How long would they wait? What if he decides he really doesn't want to try again later? What if she never got to be a mom?

Janet heard the bathroom faucet turn on and knew Marcus was up. He would normally sleep much later than this on Saturday mornings, but he didn't have that luxury on drill weekends.

She smiled up at him as he walked into the room, hoping to show in her expression that she didn't want to fight with him anymore, but he didn't even look her way as he poured coffee into his thermos.

"Good morning," she tried to sound more cheerful than she felt.

"Morning," Marcus abruptly replied. "Sorry I've gotta run. Gotta pick up Mike on my way to drill this morning."

Picking up a banana from the basket on the counter, he grabbed his keys and walked toward the front door. "Not sure what time I'll be home, so don't worry about supper," he said as he opened the door.

"I love you!" Janet called to his back and thought she heard "love you too" as the screen door snapped closed behind him.

She sat staring at the door. *Everything is going to be fine,* her inner voice assured. *He was just running late.* But Janet knew that little voice was lying, and the proof lingered in the silence. Instead of his usual kiss on her cheek, Marcus had walked out the door leaving only an ominous air of loneliness surrounding Janet as she dejectedly watched him go.

"What now?" she huffed. Most Saturdays she would go through her routine—pay bills, do some laundry, some basic chores around the house. But today wasn't the same.

He would be gone until probably supper time, so she had the whole day to herself. She thought about weeding her flowerbed, which she should do early in the morning before it got too hot outside, but she didn't feel like spending her day sweating in the heat.

Janet needed some rest, but how could she rest with the constant thought that he had made a decision that would forever change their lives?

The more she thought about it, the longer she dwelled on it, the more her sadness turned to anger.

*How dare he make a decision without thinking of me?* It made her so mad. He always did whatever *he* wanted to do. What about what she wanted out of life? When did she stop mattering to him?

Because she used to matter. What she wanted used to matter to him.

But he made it obvious that it didn't matter anymore.

Janet finished paying the bills and cleared the table. As much as she wanted to take a day off to wallow in her emotions, she knew that if she let the housework slide today, that would just be twice as much work to do tomorrow.

So she unloaded the dishwasher from the night before, started a load of laundry, made the bed, fluffed the pillows on the couch, folded up the blanket he used when he sat and watched television, then took out her cleaning supplies.

By lunch, the house was spotless, and Janet sat down on the couch to rest before starting on supper. She would cook a really nice supper to once again try to broach the subject.

*Maybe he was just having a bad day yesterday,* she hoped. *Maybe today he will actually discuss it with me.*

Janet didn't see that being likely, but it was worth a shot. She knew the lasagna recipe by heart because it was one of Marcus's favorites.

By the time he got home from drill, she would have found a better way to bring up the subject, and tonight she wasn't giving him the option of simply saying okay. Tonight, they were going to discuss the details in depth, get on the same page, and figure out what to do next.

She spent most of the afternoon thinking of ways to convince him to not give up on having a family. She would remind him of what a good dad he would be. How he always wanted to coach little league. How money wouldn't be enough to warm their hearts when they were old.

Janet took a long bath, shaving her legs and lathering a soft-scented lotion over her body. Pampering herself always boosted her energy levels. Wrapped in a towel, she debated over the clothes in her closet. She wanted to be wearing just the right outfit to help her convince Marcus he didn't want to give up on a family.

She needed a dress that was maternal, but sexy. Dressy, but not over the top. She didn't want to give him ammunition for making fun of her for dressing up for an evening at home, but she definitely needed to feel her most confident tonight, which meant looking the part.

After choosing a soft yellow sundress and white ballet-style slippers, Janet towel-dried her hair into loose waves and dabbed on a bit of lip gloss and a swipe of mascara.

She grabbed her favorite pink paisley apron from the hook on the pantry door and put it on before starting to take ingredients out of cabinets and the refrigerator to make the lasagna.

Once the lasagna was cooking, Janet tossed a nice green salad. She diced a ripe red tomato for the salad and spread butter and garlic salt over several slices of bread so they would be ready to go in the oven when she took the lasagna out to cool. Then she started washing the dishes she had dirtied already, trying to cut down on her after-dinner clean-up.

Janet stood at the kitchen sink, washing dishes, as he walked through the front door. The smell of bubbling lasagna wafted from the oven. Marcus took his military boots off and sat them by the door, then unbuttoned the uniform top as he walked toward the kitchen.

"Hey!" she turned in his direction. He responded likewise, and she continued scrubbing while he came to stand behind her awkwardly.

"What's wrong?" Janet asked nervously, sensing that something had put him in an odd mood.

"Well, the commander announced this morning that he was going to have to send four people to deploy with a unit from Kentucky. Apparently, some of their guys didn't pass the physical..."

Janet's heart thumped against her ribcage so hard she thought her bones would break. *Please don't let it be you. Please don't let them send you,* she begged silently.

"...so he asked for volunteers before he had to assign anyone to go since it's such short notice. The unit leaves the states in only two weeks."

"Well, that's good that he asked for volunteers. Thank goodness he didn't just up and tell anybody they had to pack up and go! I can't imagine how horrible it would be to get that news!" she exclaimed and shook her head with relief.

Marcus didn't say anything for a moment, but his silence screamed warning to Janet's senses. The relief she had just experienced dissipated as the panicked air whooshed from her lungs.

"You didn't," she groaned. "Please… tell me you didn't…"

Janet wished she could sink into a hole in the ground rather than stand there at the kitchen sink listening to him tell her how he had signed the paperwork already. He would leave in two weeks.

Marcus's voice remained level, though nerves shook his hands as he had explained how he felt volunteering was the right thing to do, that he'd rather it be him than one of the guys with kids, and how he hoped she would be supportive.

At the word *supportive*, her vigorous scrubs slowed, and Marcus watched her back rise and fall heavily as she took several deep breaths before taking her hands out of the suds and turning timidly around to face him.

Soapy hands dangling by her sides, she stared at him for several minutes, biting her bottom lip as the suds dripped to the linoleum floor.

"Say something," he finally prompted after waiting for her to respond to his news. Eyes closed and chin tucked, she shook her head no.

"Why won't you talk to me?" he questioned defensively. "You know we need that bonus money after all these doctor bills you've been piling up," he said, motioning to the mail on the counter beside the refrigerator.

Janet raised her head and looked at the stack of bills to which he was referring. "Bills *I've* been piling up?" she questioned, eyes still locked on the stack of envelopes.

"*We*. Bills *we've* been piling up," he backtracked.

"Look," he sighed, "we've tried and tried. If it was going to happen, it would have happened by now," he grunted. "I'm done throwing our money down the toilet for no results."

Finally, Janet turned and met his gaze. "Okay," she said, then turned to reach for the blue gingham dishtowel to dry her soapy hands, pulled it from the towel bar, and walked out of the room, carefully tiptoeing over the soapy puddles at her feet, leaving him standing in the kitchen uncertain whether he should leave her alone or follow her.

He didn't follow.

Janet went straight to the bed and curled up, fully clothed, under the sheets. *Ugh, the lasagna!* she remembered, but she didn't move. Surely he would turn the oven off.

*He volunteered.*

*He volunteered.*

*He volunteered.*

She couldn't get the thought out of her head. He was really willing to pack up and leave her. For months. No one was making him go. He volunteered.

*He would rather be at war than with me.* The tears began to flow openly, and Janet buried her head in the pillow.

She didn't know how much time passed.

Hearing the television turn off, Janet quickly rubbed her wet cheeks on the bedsheet then squeezed her eyes shut, feigning sleep as he shut the bedroom door and walked around to his side of the bed. He rolled away from her, and she listened to him breathing until he started to snore.

As stealthily as she could muster, Janet slipped out of bed to retreat to the other end of the house. She simply couldn't lie in the bed beside him like everything was okay, because it certainly was not in any way okay.

On her tip toes, Janet reached into the very back of the cabinet for a long-stemmed glass. She dusted it off with the hem of her nightshirt then stood at the island to pour herself a drink of the wine still sitting out from where she had cooked supper. Janet had refrained from drinking alcohol other than an occasional small glass with dinner since they had decided to start a family two years before.

"Guess that doesn't matter anymore," she muttered, turning the bottle up a little higher and filling her glass to the brim.

Two weeks. That's what he had said, wasn't it? Janet's heart had been pounding in her ears from the moment she heard, "I volunteered to deploy," so the details were a little fuzzy.

If all the months of trying to start a family had caused a crack in the foundation of their marriage, his volunteering to deploy would only deepen the crevasse. They had been through deployment once before when they were still newlyweds, but that was back when their love was fresh, new, full of life and hope for a future.

It was none of those things now.

She fixed herself a plate of lasagna that was sitting on the counter uncovered. He had at least taken it out of the oven. "I guess putting it in the refrigerator was too much trouble," Janet muttered, knowing she needed to put away all of the food she had prepared for a dinner they never got to eat.

She sat at the counter, eating her lasagna and sipping her wine, trying desperately to understand why he would abandon her like this.

As she looked around the room, the stars and stripes hung dauntingly above the squares on the fund-raiser calendar on the wall. She walked over to it and stared at the dates. One more day, one less empty box as she squeaked a crimson sharpie across the half-filled page. With a shaking hand, she circled the date he was scheduled to leave.

Janet stared at the numbers inside the tiny squares until tears blurred her vision. So few squares between the last X and the dreaded circle she'd just drawn.

*Is this really happening? Did he really do this to me?* Janet felt the pit in her stomach begin to bubble with rage. *He'd rather be in a freaking war zone than here with me!*

Dropping the sharpie, she snatched the calendar off the nail in the wall and flung it with all her might into the dining room where it slammed against the table before crumpling to the floor.

Hesitantly walking toward the kitchen sink with the plate and now-empty glass, she paused, contemplating the days that lay ahead. Looking back over her shoulder across the room to the calendar, tears freely flowed down Janet's cheeks and she didn't bother brushing them away.

As her hand reached to turn the faucet, the street light coming in through the window grazed the silver band on her finger. Such a short time ago, that sight would have been a comforting reassurance.

Not anymore.

The glass clanged against the stainless steel sink, shattering the silence. *One day at a time, just one day at a time,* Janet reminded herself as she turned to walk away, running a shaking hand through her hair, which was long overdue for a trim. *Time isn't something we have,* she thought, turning off the overhead kitchen lights then walking over to the couch. She curled up and wrapped herself tightly in the navy fleece blanket hugging her knees to her chest. Hoping desperately for this all to be a dream, Janet stared blankly at the popcorn ceiling.

Choking back sobs of sadness and disappointment, an overwhelming fear crashed down on her heart as she realized this upcoming good-bye might be the end of her marriage. She pulled the blanket up to her chin, buried her face in the arm of the sofa, and cried herself to sleep.

## Chapter 2

The remainder of the weekend passed in silence at home, and Marcus was happy to escape to work Monday morning. Sitting in his boss's office waiting for the older man to finish his phone call, Marcus thought about how much he would miss his job while he was gone.

"Sorry about that," the balding man apologized after hanging up the phone.

"No problem, sir," Marcus replied.

"So, how's that wife of yours doing? You guys still working on that baby?" he asked with a wink.

"Well, no, sir. Actually, I'm deploying. That's what I came to talk to you about," he cut straight to the point of their meeting before his boss asked any more questions about Janet. He explained how quickly he would be leaving, and Mr. Tremble promised that his job would be waiting for him when he returned home.

"Man, we're gonna miss you," the older man offered his hand for Marcus to shake. "How's Janet handling this? It sure seems like bad timing."

Marcus shrugged. "I guess she's okay. I think she's still processing it all."

After their conversation, Marcus shut the door to his own office down the hall and leaned against it, staring at the painting on the wall behind his desk. He knew he was running away, but this wasn't the life he agreed to. He felt like the marriage had sucked all the life out of him and he needed a change—any change—before he snapped and did something he would really regret.

He wasn't ready to give up on his marriage, but their problems were making his life miserable. All she ever talked about was having a baby. Wouldn't she rather him leave for a few months than to reach the point where he finally gave up and left permanently?

*That's not what I'm doing*, he told himself. He wasn't leaving her. Not really. He was just taking a break from their day to day problems, not their marriage. Of course, what he selfishly didn't consider was that Janet would still have to deal with the daily problems and that he was only adding to her turmoil.

Janet overworked herself for several days, trying to keep her hands busy and mind focused on menial tasks. She didn't stop for breaks at work, didn't pause to chat in the nurses' lounge, didn't lag around in the parking lot after shift. She tried hard to keep to herself and talk as little as possible. Talking about it made it real.

The way people reacted when she told them he had volunteered had not helped either. The sorrowful looks in their eyes made her sick. One of the other nurses had even broken down sobbing at the news. Janet didn't want anyone's sympathy tears.

She wanted to be angry. The hurt was easier to deal with if she focused on being mad at Marcus, which was very easy to do considering the way he was ripping her world apart and leaving her alone to piece it back together.

The distant way Marcus had been acting since his announcement helped fan the fire of Janet's anger all week long. They both tried to act as normal as possible when they went out to dinner on Friday night, but the knowledge that this was their last date for a long time hung predominantly over the whole evening.

For years, they had been making a point to go out to a nice restaurant once every couple of months. Their rule was to leave work at work and spend the evening focusing only on each other.

That rule was out the window before they even left the house this time. From the very beginning of the date, emotions were tense. Things that normally wouldn't bother Janet so much were multiplied by her stress over their situation. The little things ruined what should have been a nice evening.

Marcus always gave her a hard time for wearing high heels when they went out, and usually she took his critique as lighthearted joking. "I told you not to wear those," he'd say impertinently, his tone rubbing her attitude worse than the shoes rubbed the blisters on her tired feet. But this night, she wanted to take her shoe off and throw it at him.

She had come home early from work to get ready for the evening out. To treat herself to a little pampering to release some strain of the week before Marcus got home from work, Janet had taken a long soak in the whirlpool tub with lavender scented bubbles, shaved her legs and lathered on the soft, thick cherry blossom lotion that tingled her tanned skin. She painted her nails and toes a vibrant pink that matched the one-shouldered dress she'd been waiting for a special occasion to wear, then picked out her sexiest heels and strapped them on.

As she had stood in front of the full-length mirror that hung at the back of the closet door smoothing the front of the dress with her hands and hoping he would notice the effort she'd put forth and tell her she looked beautiful, Marcus had stood in the bedroom, rambling on about one of his clients without so much as a glance in her direction. He'd been so preoccupied for months that he rarely noticed her or ever truly looked at her.

While they sat at the dinner table trying to enjoy a good steak, she hadn't brought up the issue of deployment, so neither had he. However, Marcus had noticed that the dark circles under her eyes made her look older than her thirty years and felt a twinge of guilt because he knew he was to blame.

What Marcus hadn't noticed that week was the calendar crumpled in the trash or the empty wine glass drying in the dish rack night after night. He didn't notice the bottle of expensive prenatal vitamins in the trash underneath the bathroom sink along with the parenting magazines that had been kept on her side of the bed for months.

By the time the date finally ended, they were both glad. They made love as they normally would on date night, but the physical connection was greatly diminished by the emotional void dividing them.

By Sunday morning, Janet was just about ready for him to leave. She remembered from the first deployment that waiting for him to go could sometimes be worse than him actually being gone. The dread was worse than the loneliness.

The unspoken fears dampened the mood over their Sunday morning breakfast before church. However, if Janet was being honest, long before deployment became an issue, those Sunday breakfasts had become colder just as the space between them on the pew had widened.

As she sat at the table with him before Sunday School, Janet hardly spoke a word, cutting her pancakes into tiny pieces, then drenching each bite in maple syrup. As always finishing before he would, Janet read her Sunday School lesson while twirling her fingers around the tarnished cross necklace she'd worn for years.

When he had scraped the last bit of syrup from his plate, he mumbled "thank you" as she quietly cleaned off the table. She started washing the dishes while he changed into his church clothes.

Marcus blamed himself for the change that had come over her Sunday morning at the breakfast table. He had been commanded by God to be the head of their household, the loving spiritual leader of their home, and he had failed in that area. In the biggest decision of their lives so far, he had not even consulted God and God's will—only Marcus's wants and Marcus's frustrations did he take into consideration.

They drove to church in silence, each acutely aware that today would be difficult. Everyone in the congregation would want to hug Marcus or shake his hand. Then they would each turn to Janet with a pitiful smile and tell her to call if she needed anything.

The preacher's sermon was about miracles, how Jesus multiplied the fish and bread, turned the water into wine, healed the blind man.

Janet shivered and reached under the seat for the blanket she kept there week to week. No matter what the temperature was outside, that old church was always either too hot or too cold, which caused some distraction for Janet and grumbling from Marcus as they sat in the olive-colored cushioned pew every Sunday. In the winter, the heater would blast him out of the sanctuary while she'd be wrapped in the blanket. In the ninety-degree summer, they'd both have to bring a light jacket because the old ladies would have the air conditioner set on sixty.

The Bible they shared sat across Marcus's thigh where they could both read the passages along with the sermon, until the invitation hymn began to play at the end of the service.

As anticipated, Marcus and Janet didn't get back in their car until thirty minutes after the service had ended. Janet's throat ached from choking back sobs and trying to smile like she had everything together.

Janet guessed she had been hugged at least fifty times in the last hour.

"Oh, honey, don't you worry. He'll be fine," one little old lady comforted Janet. Many others expressed similar reassurances, but Janet couldn't explain to them that she wasn't worried about his health. She was worried about their marriage.

A few of the men patted her on the shoulder without saying a word, little kids hugged her legs, and women her age just smiled while keeping their distance. No one knew exactly how to react, which Janet remembered from her first experience with deployment.

This time was different, though. The news came so suddenly that people were shocked. Janet felt them all looking at her oddly. She thought she could sense their wonderings: *I wonder why he volunteered. Are they having money troubles? Is there some reason he wants to leave her? I thought they were trying to have a baby.*

With every hand shake, Janet felt the speculations sizing up her situation, and she didn't like it. She was tapping her toe, anxious to leave while waiting on Marcus. Everyone else had finally left the churchyard, and Janet stood by the locked car waiting for Marcus to return with the keys.

Even Marcus seemed a little shaken up as they drove home. Janet watched him behind the steering wheel out of the corner of her eye, wondering what the preacher had said to him when the two men had wandered off for several minutes.

But his thoughts were a mystery to her, his expressions unreadable, as though she didn't know him at all anymore.

The day Marcus was scheduled to fly out, he and Janet stood in the bedroom trying to pack the last of his luggage. Antipathy and frustration lurked throughout the room with each item that went in the bags, much unlike the day they packed for his first deployment.

Before the first deployment, she'd sat on the bed reading off his packing list over and over again, triple checking to make sure he had everything he needed. Today, Janet's attitude was one of defeat before the challenge even began. She'd sat a laundry basket full of clean clothes and underwear by his suitcase on the bed alongside his packing list, making sure he had everything he needed.

She couldn't help put the clothes in the bags, though. Years in the military had taught him exactly how to pack as much as possible in one bag, so it worked better if she just let him do it his way.

Watching him pack his suitcase to leave, Janet didn't feel as though he were packing for a deployment. The heartbreak she experienced seemed more like he was just leaving her for good.

Her heart pounded in her ears and she knew she better take some medicine now or she would have a terrible headache by the end of the day.

"Have you seen my laptop cord?" he asked. Janet walked into the living room and came back with it, sitting it on the bed by his suitcase.

"Thanks," he said quietly.

When she didn't say anything in response, Marcus looked up from packing to meet her tear-filled gaze.

"Come here," he said gently. Janet fell into his arms and he held her tightly against his chest. "Shhh, baby. It's going to be okay."

Janet sobbed hard into his shirt and fought the urge to hit him in the chest for making her feel this pain. "I just don't understand," she choked.

"Understand what?" he questioned.

"Why you don't want me anymore," Janet whispered between sobs.

"Hey, hey, shh," he consoled. "What makes you think I don't want you?"

Janet just shook her head because she couldn't explain. And if she tried to, it would likely result in an argument, which she didn't want to start.

The cab driver in the driveway honked his horn announcing his arrival.

Janet pulled away from Marcus and brushed the tears from her eyes. She smoothed her hands across the cotton fabric of her dress and began to pick up a bag to carry to the car. Marcus followed her toting the other two bags.

While he loaded them into the trunk, she ran back inside to grab her purse and keys. Settled uncomfortably in the back seat of the cab with her purse in her lap, Janet's knees bounced with nervous energy as she stared out the window.

Marcus reached over and gently put his hand over her knee.

Her eyes dropped to where his hand rested, and she covered his with her own. Hand in hand, they rode to the airport in silence. Janet held her back as straight as possible, fighting the urge to slump and hang her head so her hair would hide the tears rolling down her cheeks. She squeezed his hand and let the teardrops fall all the way to the airport drop off where the cab slowly stopped and Marcus patted her knee.

Watching Marcus in his civilian clothes checking in two big green duffles, the difference between this and his first deployment flashed in her mind again. When he deployed the first time, the bleachers of the high school gym had been filled with family members of the dozens of soldiers lined up in uniform on the gym floor.

But this time, not a single family member had been given enough notice to be able to get off work. They had all come over the night before to tell him bye, so today she was on her own. She had to say goodbye then go home to an empty house. Although today she would be telling him good-bye just as she did all those years ago, standing in the airport alone watching him board the plane would be a completely different experience than standing outside the school on the grass with the other wives watching the greyhound buses pull out of the parking lot. She wasn't alone that day. She didn't have to drive home to an empty house because her parents had insisted on bringing her back to stay with them for the weekend.

She tried not to get separated by the crowd as she followed him through the terminal. The airport was fairly small, and she was able to go all the way to the gate to sit in the waiting area with him. She remembered that deployment meant a lot of waiting. Waiting. And waiting. Months of waiting.

"It won't be forever," he said, interrupting her thoughts.

"I know." Janet wiped a tear away and sniffled.

Marcus put his arm around her shoulders and pulled her in close, slowly rocking her back and forth. As Marcus sat there holding her, Janet thought back over how different they were now than they were when they first went through this type of trial together.

A mere six months into their marriage—before the young couple had gotten a chance to get settled into their new home and learn each other's quirks—his National Guard unit had notified them of the upcoming deployment to the Middle East. With six months to prepare, they'd made the most of every minute possible, taking day-cations and weekend getaways whenever they could. They gushed about how much they'd miss each other, how often they'd write, what he would want shipped in care packages, and, most of all, how their love for each other was strong enough to handle anything.

Neither of them had any clue what lay in store for them in the months that would follow. She promised to write often, to send care packages, to take pictures of everything going on at home so he wouldn't miss anything big or small, but Janet learned quickly that keeping those promises was much harder than she had anticipated.

But she had put forth the extra effort, stayed up late boxing up Vienna sausages, outdoorsman magazines, and used DVDs from the $2 bin at the local movie rental store. She'd baked his favorite chocolate chip cookies and double-wrapped them in cellophane to ship in a special package once a month. She had taken pictures of every new decoration she bought for their house and of every flower she planted in the front yard and included those prints in his boxes.

Love alone wasn't enough to get them through that first big test; a lot of effort was given to keep their bond strong.

Maybe this second goodbye was harder because they knew exactly what to expect, or in Janet's case, exactly what to dread. Leading up to this second separation with only two weeks to prepare, they didn't talk much about being apart or missing each other; instead, they covered little more than the basic logistics— what day to take out the trash, whom to call when the grass needed cutting, how to access and manage his accounts, when the oil needed to be changed in his truck, what day of the month the house payment was due—nothing intimate like they had before on his first overseas departure.

Marcus sat with his arm around her until twenty minutes later when his row was called over the loud speaker to board. They exchanged *I love you's* and shared one long, heartfelt kiss, and Janet didn't want to let go.

As Marcus walked through the gate and turned back to offer her a sad smile and raise his hand to wave, Janet held her fists tightly clenched at her sides and bit her bottom lip, not daring to breathe until he was out of sight.

In a matter of seconds, he turned and was gone.

She slowly turned toward the ladies room and pushed through the heavy door. Luckily, the entire facility was empty, although she realized as she crumbled to the cold tile that it wouldn't have mattered if there had been standing room only. Tears of fear and anguish poured so desperately that no tissue could soak them up quickly enough.

# Chapter 3

With her makeup reapplied to camouflage the redness of her cheeks, Janet exited the airport bathroom. With a stern look of determination, she headed straight for the airport bar.

Feeling numb, she sat down at the bar and ordered without even glancing at the menu. The bartender brought Janet a glass of wine and side salad within a matter of minutes, and Janet stared blankly at a baseball game on one of the televisions above the bar while she ate.

Janet didn't notice when one ballgame on television ended and another one started. She just stared for what seemed like hours at the screen.

"Is this seat taken?" a deep voice asked hopefully, his three-piece suit straight out of a magazine, collar unbuttoned and burgundy tie loosened. She took another sip, averting her eyes to the food on her plate.

"I'm waiting on someone," Janet replied, not daring to meet the gaze of the man standing by her table so close she could smell the faint musky aroma of his aftershave.

"My apologies," the stranger replied regretfully. "Enjoy your evening." As the gentleman walked away, Janet twirled the white gold ring on her left hand, feeling lonelier now than before. She hadn't told him a total lie. She *was* waiting for someone, but he was much too far away for an evening dinner any night soon.

His plane hadn't been gone long, and she'd be waiting much longer before he would finally arrive home from his extended business trip and twenty-hour flight from the damned sandbox, his three-piece suit finished off not with polished oxfords but rather with combat boots.

Janet, fidgeting while still trying to avoid the gaze of the well-dressed gentleman who now sat across the room, reached into the multi-colored flowered shoulder bag—one of several recent purchases in a string of attempts to brighten her days—to pull out the cell phone she knew would soon become her best friend.

The evening strolled on uneventfully, unless, of course, she counted the hole being bored into her back by the gentleman's poignant stares. She wondered if he'd taken his eyes off her during his entire meal. From the corner of her eye, she could see him sitting at a table with two other gentlemen who never seemed to notice that the direction of his attention wasn't aimed at their conversation.

Once, she accidently made the mistake of meeting the gentleman's gaze. Janet quickly broke eye contact and diverted her attention to digging into her purse.

If only Marcus had looked at her like that even once in the year before he left, the loving look he used to give her earlier in their marriage when they had shared the same hopes and worked collectively toward their mutual dreams.

*When did his dreams change?* Janet wondered as she sipped the glass of wine the bartender had just refilled. The months of fertility treatments had been hard on both of them, but she had been willing to do whatever it took to help God along in starting their family. She had always believed that God wouldn't have given her such a strong desire for motherhood unless he intended her to be a mother. The possibility of never having children had never crossed her mind, but then after months and months of trying to no avail, the doctor confirmed one of her worst nightmares, and the awful process of being poked and prodded had begun.

Marcus had seemed supportive at first. He had done his part and helped her with the daily injections, but somewhere during the two years of failed attempts and financial strain of the treatments, he became stressed. Janet had thought he was simply frustrated because he had wanted a child so badly, so the sudden announcement of his new decision to not have kids had been an absolute shock, a devastating blow to her dreams. The small window of opportunity to which she'd been clinging slammed closed in her face. He chose to give up and had given her no options other than to deal with it or leave.

She motioned to the bartender for her check then reached for her purse. Her long hair fell in front of her face when she bent over, so she didn't see the man who walked up to take the seat next to her.

But she sensed him immediately. Maybe it was the wine, but the man who sat down next to her took her breath away.

As she sat upright, she brushed her hair behind her ear.

"Hi. Do I know you?" the handsome man asked with an inquisitive gaze.

Janet looked in his blue eyes and thought they seemed familiar. "I'm not sure. I'm Janet," she stuck out her hand.

He slowly wrapped his hand around hers in a firm handshake, "I thought so! I'm Russ. You work at my mom's nursing home."

"Oh, yes!" she recognized him immediately once he made that connection for her. He came by at least once every week for lunch and a group of the nurses always swooned over him. Janet had seen him on a regular basis for months although they'd never spoken.

"Surely your date didn't stand you up," the tall stranger commented, his blue eyes prying into hers, obviously trying to determine why they were tear-brimmed and blood-shot.

"Something like that," she replied noncommittally, shrugging her shoulders.

"Well, don't rush off. Have a drink with me." He smiled.

"Thank you, Russ"—she emphasized his name with a nod—"but I can't. I need to get home."

Russ smiled and shook his head. "He must not know how lucky he is if he's standing you up, but very well," he said with a tip of his head.

Janet smiled shyly and politely mumbled her thanks.

Despite turning him down on his offer for a drink, Janet remained seated even after paying her tab. Russ told her about the business trip he had been on, making one-sided small talk since Janet obviously didn't seem very talkative herself.

Janet enjoyed listening to him talk, and she really enjoyed the way he actually looked at her when he spoke. Marcus hardly ever looked at her. He would focus on the newspaper, television, or on his food when they talked – rarely on her.

When she took the last sip of her wine, Russ downed the last of his drink as well.

"Well, I think it's about time for me to head on home," he said as he began to stand. "Would you like me to walk you to your car?"

Janet also began to stand, but her feet weren't as sturdy as his, so he offered an arm for her to steady herself. "I didn't drive," she admitted.

"Well, that's a good thing!" his eyes widened as he gave the bartender a stern look of reproach. He obviously thought Janet had been served one glass of wine too many. "Here, I'll help you hail a cab."

Janet wasn't in the mood to argue with him and allowed him to lead her from the restaurant. She couldn't remember the last time she'd drank like this and was glad someone was there to make sure she was okay.

As she stepped through the doorway into the night air, his free hand courteously grazed the small of her back as if guiding her through the exit. As soon as she felt his touch, it was gone, yet the chill-bumps spreading across Janet's limbs weren't from the cold as she walked through the terminal toward the line of cabs outside.

Over the years, Janet had felt her common beauty fading. Her features weren't supermodel material, and she would never be a Cover Girl, but what she didn't realize was how the extra pounds she'd gained over the years had spread out impeccably in the eyes of many men. Her skinny legs and tiny waist had transformed into luscious curves that even the objectionable scrubs she hid behind most days couldn't veil. The curvature of her hips when she walked was such that any red-blooded man, not unlike the well-dressed gentleman at her side, couldn't help but notice.

Russ hailed a cab and opened the door for her. As she slipped into the back seat, a flicker of excitement crawled through her veins.

"Are you sure you're going to be okay going home? I can ride along with you if you'd like," he offered politely.

As he leaned over the car door as though to convince himself she wasn't lying, she assured him she was fine and thanked him for walking her to a cab.

"Anything I can do to help a pretty lady," he smiled. "Could I see you again?"

"I appreciate your interest, but I'm not available," she declared firmly. She paused before elaborating, "I'm married."

He smiled again. "That's no surprise," he confessed, noticing the way she cocked her head to the side at his admission. "I'd be more surprised if you weren't."

Janet blushed at his obvious compliment and averted her gaze.

"I shall leave you since you're a happily married woman," he declared as he pushed himself back from the cab.

When he was a step away from the door, he halted and turned to face Janet who sat in the back seat unmoving. His gaze locked with hers.

"You are *happily* married, right?" he asked, emphasizing the word *happily* then flashed another million-dollar smile in her direction before closing the door, leaving her alone to contemplate her answer.

In the beam of the porch light, her front door looked lonely as the cab pulled up to her driveway. Sighing, she grabbed her colorful new purse and flung it over her shoulder as she opened the car door and stepped out onto the pavement, the click of her heels echoing loudly across the hushed night air.

Janet slowly started walking toward the back door of their quaint ranch-style home, the suffocating silence to which she had been dreading return.

Not quite ready to enter the empty house, she turned instead to the gate to the backyard and walked over toward the wooden swing below the canopy of the oak tree. By the dim glow of the porch light, she tiptoed through the dry grass while trying to keep the heels of her shoes from sinking onto the parched dirt. The southeastern part of Mississippi where Janet and Marcus lived had experienced its driest summer in years, and Janet couldn't bring herself to waste water in running a sprinkler just to water her grass. She did at least water her garden once a day, but only just enough and not a drop more to keep the leaves on her tomatoes from wilting.

*It's not like other people see how pitiful the grass looks anyway since I'm the only one ever around,* she thought begrudgingly of the neighbors chasing their kids through a sprinkler in their lush backyard while she sat at home conserving water. The crunching blades beneath her feet didn't appreciate her frugality.

As she sat down, she brushed a few leaves from the seat of the swing before smoothing the soft cotton dress underneath her. One by one, she unclasped the buckle on each high-heeled shoe and sat it on the ground beside her. She always got so mad when Marcus scolded her about wearing those, and, even though she'd never admit it, she knew he was right. But when they would get ready to go out, she just couldn't bear the thought of missing the opportunity to wear cute shoes as opposed to her usual nursing flats.

Her poor feet, however, didn't bode well after a night in heels, which mocked the comfort her feet had become accustomed to on a daily basis. There was definitely something to be said for nursing shoes—they were comfortable even after several hours of trips back and forth down the halls during a shift. One trek down the corridor in heels would have her searching for a Band-Aid.

Janet turned her back against the arm of the wooden swing and pulled her knees to her chest. Her arms instinctively wrapped around her bare legs as she leaned against the back of the swing, her left cheek resting on the cold wood.

As she stared at the trunk of that old oak tree, her eyes clouded over with stubborn tears, remembering the first time she'd lain eyes on its towering branches on that crisp November day ten years before. Marcus had been looking at houses to rent when his current lease ended in December, and he'd brought her along to get her opinion. They'd started dating the previous summer and had quickly come to rely on each other's opinions for everything—from which milkshake flavor to order (birthday cake was her favorite flavor; butter pecan was his) to which car insurance to buy.

She'd been charmed, although not overwhelmed, by the cute guest bedroom and dual sinks in the master bath, but didn't see why he needed so much space in a rental. *It must have been a bargain he couldn't resist*, she'd thought at the time. As they'd toured the rooms, Janet had tried to keep her mind from mentally contemplating paint colors and other cosmetic improvements. The house needed a lot of tender loving care to eliminate the dated bachelor-pad appearance. After all, this would be *his* house, not *hers*, so she'd thought.

He had taken her hand, intertwining his fingers with hers, and led her into the backyard.

She hadn't been too impressed by the squeak of the sliding glass door that didn't want to slide, nor of the duct tape over the torn screen as she had stepped out onto a worn patio.

"I'm thinking we'll put a nice swing right here," he'd said with a smile while spreading his arms out in front of him and walking toward the big oak tree. "Maybe one day a playhouse and sandbox over there." He nodded toward the corner of the yard.

His suggestions had completely caught Janet off guard. Her feet froze, her heart skipped, and her thoughts faltered. Did he really just mean what she thought he did?

Growing up, Janet, like every other little girl, had imagined her prince asking for her hand in marriage and how excited she would be when that day finally came. She had twirled around in one of her mom's lacey white dresses pretending she was a princess, marched down the hallway toward her childhood bedroom humming "Here Comes the Bride" carrying a bundle of plastic roses her dad had picked up for her at the Dollar Store while envisaging the flutter of her heart when she held out her hand for the prince to place the ring on her finger.

The big moment was nothing like she imagined. He actually never said the words, "Will you marry me?" Marcus had simply walked toward her, smiling brightly as he pulled the ring box from the pocket of his blue jeans.

As Marcus had gently kissed the diamond he placed on her ring finger, no fireworks exploded in the air; no cheers or whistles erupted from the peasants in the courtyard below; no blinding excitement rushed through her. In fact, it was surprisingly quite the opposite.

In that moment, Janet felt more peaceful than she had at any other instance prior or since. She knew without question that this house was her home, and this man was the prince with whom she'd share it. Everything was right. Complete.

Ten years later, sitting under that same tree in the swing he'd hung for her the day they'd moved in, Janet longed to feel that peace again. The years of failing to start a family had taken a toll on their relationship. Coupled with the financial and emotional drain from the constant treatments, the disappointment was amplified by time apart for military reasons—missed anniversaries, missed birthdays, missed Christmases, time they could never get back. *Sacrifice for the greater good*, he always reminded her.

Janet understood that sacrifice was necessary for freedom to be protected, and she was not opposed to it. When she first married Marcus, she had known she must be willing to sacrifice time with her husband as well as her sense of shelter while he was away and the financial security of his civilian job for the low salary of a soldier overseas during deployments. Other than the dreaded possibility no military wife wants to contemplate about her husband never coming home, the young Janet had no clue how devastating the sacrifices the military life would require of her.

Since he had announced his deployment, some days she blamed Marcus for giving up on their family; some days she blamed the military for offering him an easy way out.

Having already been through one deployment, Janet knew starting this second tour that she had to be tough from day one.

She had been so strong when he first deployed. Standing at the airport watching him board the plane, she had gritted her teeth into a forced smile, demanding the tears to stay at bay. She did not want him to see her cry as he turned away. She didn't want the image of tears rolling down her cheeks to be burned into his memory.

She was resilient. She was strong. She could handle this.

The slight late-summer breeze gently rocked the swing, and Janet blinked heavily, forcing the tears back into their hidden place, determining them not to fall. She knew that one tear just led to more, and that there'd be no stopping the waterfall once it began.

She would not cry.

The next two days, Janet was surprisingly able to go to work like normal. Those couple days were actually pretty good with none of the usual work chaos while, unbeknownst to Janet, her coworkers were orchestrating every aspect of her shift from behind the scenes.

The National Guard had been calling Marcus away one weekend a month and two weeks a year throughout their entire relationship, so Janet had spent a lot of weekends at home without him over the years, which made her accustomed to a couple days here and there of being alone at the house. Those first few days of this second deployment had basically seemed to be one of those drill weekends or the start of summer camp training.

Marcus wasn't able to call the first two days while he was getting settled at the base where he'd be prepped for a week before going overseas, but Janet was used to that. He often wouldn't call when he was away at drill overnight; therefore, two days without a call from him didn't shake her resolve.

Even if it might have shaken her, Janet didn't allow herself time to be dazed. When she got home from work each day, she stayed busy. Janet caught up on housework she had left undone in the two weeks prior to deployment, and the impact of Marcus's absence did not hit her squarely until days after their goodbye at the airport.

She recalled from his first overseas deployment the importance of staying active; the first year apart had been difficult, but as a practically new wife, she took advantage of the extra free time to start building their future together by investing time and careful thought into their home.

Now, Marcus being gone really didn't upset her routine too much. They hardly did anything together other than watch television. In some respects, her workload would actually be lessened by fewer clothes, fewer dishes, and no one to cook for. So Janet stuck to her routine until the third night Marcus was gone. He had left on a Monday, and now it was Wednesday. She had done a good job blocking out the stress and pain until then.

They usually went to church on Wednesday nights, so she came home from work and began to change clothes after tossing her scrubs in the closet. After taking a shower, she had sat down at her laptop for a few minutes before getting dressed for prayer meeting. An email from Marcus greeted her:

"Just got in from the training field. Headed to supper. Won't have much time to talk tonight, but I'll call after supper. Love you," she read.

Foregoing church for the night in hopes of stealing a few minutes of his time, Janet had adorned her pajamas and sat on the couch intending to spend some time browsing the websites of her favorite magazines. This was something she loved to do but rarely allowed time for because of Marcus's opinion that browsing through magazines was a waste of time. Rather than get upset when he teased her about it or have her feelings hurt by his reprimand, Janet usually circumvented any possibility of quarrel by relinquishing the pastimes he thought were silly, meaning no magazines while he was around. She usually saved those for her "Me time" during Marcus's drill weekends.

As soon as she had settled in on the cushions, propped her feet up on the oak coffee table and sat her laptop across her thighs, Janet opened the computer and got ready to dive into months of unread home décor articles and tasty recipes. As she had guided the cursor to the search box, her fingers became immobile on the keys.

He wasn't there to tease her or condemn her for wasting time. Janet stalled.

In that moment, with hands poised on the keyboard with the expectation of months of long evenings lounging on the sofa browsing new recipes she would love to try but had no one to taste test and the hundreds of backdated magazines she would have time to read, the lonely reality she had been avoiding finally overwhelmed her.

And Janet had fallen apart.

Regardless of the distance that had developed between them, Janet still missed his presence. Despite his habitual teasing, his patronizing remarks, his detached attitude prior to deployment, she still wanted to hear his voice.

For the next few weeks, she was so distraught she could hardly function. She even had to take a couple days off work because she couldn't unwrap herself from the snug cocoon of her down comforter. Those first couple of months, she had cried after every conversation with him and every time she lay down in bed to feign sleep, and crying hurt all over. Her face was always swollen, her eyes always burned, and her ribs ached from sobbing.

No one in Janet's life understood why she was so upset, and she couldn't explain it. Her family and few close friends at work thought her reaction to his deployment was too dramatic. They didn't believe she could be as upset as she seemed.

They didn't know how tense their home life had gotten before deployment, how she'd been holding in these feelings for months and that deployment was just the breaking point to what she could handle. No one knew that she had been struggling to hold her head up at work and home for at least a year. In the year before Marcus left, Janet's coworkers saw her work ethic become better than ever; her positive attitude toward her patients overcompensating for the attention she wasn't getting at home. Her family saw Janet holding Marcus's hand as they bowed their heads before Sunday lunch but didn't realize that that small gesture was the only physical contact the couple made in weeks.

No one except Marcus and her doctor had even known she'd been taking fertility treatments. When she hadn't become pregnant, she was ever more thankful not to have to see their sympathetic smiles or hear the empty encouragement they would have offered had they known the extent to which they'd been trying.

When Marcus left, Janet had stopped pretending. All attempts to feign happiness and normalcy left with him, and she gave in to the dark cloud that had been hanging over her head unnoticed by others for months.

Not knowing what was wrong or why she had taken this deployment so hard, her coworkers weren't sure how to broach the subject of her puffy eyes; her mom kept telling her to perk up while her dad looked on with a worried expression; and her doctor, when she'd gone for help because she felt sickly and weak all the time, had diagnosed her as clinically depressed and prescribed antidepressants that he said would help her sleep and manage her moods.

Janet refused to think of herself as depressed, so she hadn't filled the prescription. The term "depression" seemed too serious for her situation—a woman alone for one year. Nothing tragic had happened to her—no death in the family, no natural disaster had destroyed everything she owned, no layoff from her job, no foreclosure of her home like many other people across the country were facing—so she couldn't be depressed in every sense of the word as she understood it.

She just knew that her heart physically ached, her chest felt tight like she was pinned underneath a mound of debris, her muscles painfully rebelled against her normal routine, her thought processes seemed muddled, and her eyes begged incessantly for sleep. Then one day, Janet suddenly decided she was tired of crying and feeling down about herself.

She wasn't sure where her epiphany came from, but Janet determined that life would be easier if she disregarded the pain, shut off her sentiments, and went on with her routine. The ache was still ever-present throughout her body and soul, but her mind resolutely blocked it out.

She hadn't cried since.

# *Chapter 4*

*Deep breaths. In through the nose. Out through the mouth. In. Out.*

After a long week, the idea of heating up another frozen dinner sickened Janet's stomach, so when her coworkers had invited her to join them on a Thursday girls night, she had jumped at the opportunity to treat herself to a night out. But had she anticipated they would one by one leave early in the evening and that she would end up sitting at a table alone trying to project an air of contentment, Janet probably would have stayed home and forced down a tray of bland pasta like she did most nights.

Susie had announced early in the evening that she would have to leave in time to put her kids to bed. So after she left, Janet thought she and Liz would stay and hang out for a while longer. But Liz got a call from her on again/off again beau and rushed to meet him before he changed his mind.

Leaving Janet alone.

As usual.

*There you go. Just take it easy,* she thought to herself hoping the young couple at the next high-top did not notice her anxious concentration. Why was she worrying what they thought about her nervousness? It wasn't as though they could hear her thoughts over the ten flat screen televisions, all on different channels, blasting out above the liquor bottles framing the bar—assuming their eyes ever unlocked, anyway. Young love.

*Just wait ten years,* Janet thought rolling her eyes, thinking of how much her own marriage used to resemble that young pair—gazing into each other's eyes, smiling so hard their cheeks must hurt, affectionately hanging on each other's every word. Look where that had gotten her—months and months of seemingly endless nights alone while he was away. Again.

She concentrated on taking slow deep breaths. In *two three*, out *two three*, she counted, closing her eyes for a moment. Her anxiety level had reached unknown heights of late, and the stress was affecting many aspects of Janet's health. Her doctor, concerned with her blood pressure levels, had suggested yoga or pilates to channel her pent-up energy and release her stress. *Sure, Doc, let me pencil that in my wide open schedule,* she had thought sarcastically while sitting on the examination table. As though her home life wasn't difficult enough right now, work had been especially trying on her mentally, physically, and spiritually. The compilation of all of it weighed heavily on her heart day and night.

Some days were harder than others. Today was one of those days. Janet's patients, lonely and longing to escape their helpless situations, must have sensed her own yearning to escape the suffocating white walls of the nursing home. Some days those patients were her haven, her reason for wearing the unflattering scrubs rather than her favorite fluffy pink slippers. But on days like today, they broke her heart.

Mrs. Tanner's husband had come to visit that morning. Usually, Mrs. Tanner would at least recognize her husband, even though she didn't know what decade they were living in, but today Mrs.

Tanner had no clue who he was. He had patiently sat beside her, trying to reassure her that forgetting was okay, but Janet could see the agony in the old man's brown eyes from how his wife's relentless disease was ripping away a treasured part of his heart.

Mrs. Tanner rarely recognized her children because, to her, they were still in elementary school, not the middle-aged adults who came in her room calling her "Mom." In truth, Mrs. Tanner's children's children already had children of their own. Janet's soul ached for the woman, who had lived long enough to see her great-grandchildren but couldn't recall their existence.

Although Janet had no children of her own, she could not begin to imagine not remembering her daughter's wedding day, being unable to recall nervously adjusting her daughter's white lace veil—a veil she'd spend tedious hours sewing by hand—or straightening her husband's bowtie before the ceremony began and watching him walk their baby girl down the aisle.

Losing a lifetime of precious memories was terrible, but Janet knew that the loved ones who still had their memories seemed to be the ones who hurt the most. Janet's fragile heart broke over and over again for Mrs. Tanner and her family. Watching someone suffer like that and lose so many important pieces of her life was almost more than Janet's nerves could bear.

The thoughts of Mrs. Tanner's battle with dementia caused guilt to rush over Janet. While she spent her days trying desperately to block the pre-deployment memories just to ease the ache in her heart—an ache that burned deeper than she could have ever imagined—she witnessed daily the ache that resulted from memories lost forever.

Mrs. Tanner had stared blankly at her husband Tom that morning as he calmly stroked her hand and babbled excitedly about the antics of their eleven-month-old great-grandson who was running around and keeping their grandson Jack and his wife Linda on their toes. She had barely even glanced at the crisp photo he pulled out of his wallet and tacked on the bulletin board in her room that was blanketed in family photos in hopes of triggering a memory, which sadly only happened on rare occasions.

Taking another bitter sip from the goblet in her hand, biting the flavor and savoring it on her tongue, Janet recognized that comfort came in all forms—for Mrs. Tanner, it came in photos with the hopes of regaining memories; for Janet, today it came in a long-stemmed glass with the hopes of forgetting—but who could find comfort surrounded by sadness all day and coming home to an empty house and the six o'clock news? It was the same old stories, same old war that seemed as though it would never end.

And she hadn't heard from Marcus in several days, long, horrible, agonizing days. Weeks like this, rarely hearing from him at all, were becoming more routine, and no news was not always good news when it came to being a military wife.

While she missed him tremendously, the little voice in the back of her mind consistently reminded her that he chose to leave, tinting all pining for him with bitterness. He knowingly chose to leave her here to fend for herself, and, however honorable and noble his sacrifice was, he still chose that life over the one she had always dreamed they would have—the white picket fence, two kids riding their pink and blue bicycles along the sidewalk to go play with the neighbors, and family dinners around the table each night.

Instead, Janet had somehow ended up as a thirty-year-old lonely woman eating dinner alone, usually standing over the sink or sitting on the couch watching pointless television. At least tonight, she'd gotten out of the house and wasn't wearing sweatpants.

Eating alone wasn't fun. Sure, she had eaten alone when she was out running errands around lunchtime and stopped somewhere for a quick bite or when she needed a real break from work and took a long lunch off premises in her scrubs. Tonight, sitting at the table after her coworkers went home to their lives, was much different. At least they had invited her out in the first place because her friends never did. Tonight was supposed to be about instilling a little life back into her wearisome world, but here she sat alone. As usual.

Janet had spent most of the last several months cooped up in their ranch-style home in their quiet neighborhod cul-de-sac, but the walls had lately begun closing in on her. She needed to escape from the lonely house and wished she had a friend who would go to the movies or have dinner with her, but all of her "friends" were too wrapped up in their own lives—their husbands and kids—to acknowledge Janet's loneliness or need for camaraderie.

Janet did not want to believe that her friends were aware of her feelings and just didn't care, yet she was forced to recognize that she obviously didn't cross their minds very often. Maybe they didn't call because they didn't know what to say, or maybe they genuinely didn't have two minutes to spare, or maybe they thought she was tough enough to handle the deployment without any outside support. Whatever their reasons were, her friends never called, never invited her to their girls' night out, never texted, never even sent her messages on Facebook anymore, and she didn't know why.

She couldn't really blame them. She hadn't called them either, but she didn't have anything positive to talk about, and, truth be told, she didn't want to hear about their happy lives while she was so miserable. With her own self-centered tendencies, Janet couldn't see that her own negativity and self-loathing were likely the culprit for the failed relationships. Her weak self-esteem caused her to always expect people to disappoint her, deprioritize her, or dismiss her. Janet did not realize that she was often the one doing these things to herself.

The friendships had started drifting apart long before deployment when Janet's friends all started having children and she didn't. She and Marcus just hadn't been in the rush that other couples their age seemed to be in when it came to starting a family. While she was content with their decision early in their marriage to wait before having children, the results made her an outsider.

She often wondered who pulled away from whom first. Had her friends pulled away to spend more time with their growing families, or had she pulled away so they *could* spend more time with their growing families? She didn't know. It had happened so fast. One day she was out to coffee, slowly sipping her mocha latte, when her best friend smiled exuberantly as she shared her big news with Janet. Soon, Janet, feeling like an intruder, was quietly backing out of the hospital room as her friend's family crowded around the new baby. Her friend had become a mom, and, rightfully so, everything had changed.

One by one, Janet's college friends had started families. They hung out with other moms, not with Janet, and she understood. Progressively, she had less and less in common with them. Their lives were completely different. Her friends were just thinking about teething, potty training, first haircuts, day care, Easter Bunny, Santa Claus, and the list of differences grew even more every year.

But didn't they know how supportive she would've been had they given her the chance? Didn't they know that she would love to be invited to their kids' birthday parties, to help decorate Easter eggs, to even babysit on occasion? Not having children of her own, Janet experienced a loneliness she couldn't explain and often wondered how she could miss something she'd never had. Not having friends, or even family who understood, only added to her loneliness.

She had tried once to talk to her sister about wanting children, but Julia had brushed it off and gone on a tangent about crayon on the walls and stepping on baby dolls in every room.

Thinking of family, Janet could at least count on hers when she really needed them, even if she couldn't turn to them for advice or confide in them her deepest pains. For the first few months of deployment, someone had called to check on her nearly every day, and it could either be her mom, her dad, her sister, or one of her aunts or cousins. At that point, Janet had thanked God for giving her a big family instead of a lot of friends, and she told herself daily in an effort to ease the pain of vanished friendships that family was better, anyway. Blood is thicker than water, as her grandmother had often reminded Janet and her sister every time they got into squabbles as children.

The phone calls had gradually slowed to every other day, then down to every few days, then slowed down to once a week until eventually, everyone except her mom had stopped calling. Sometimes her mom would put her dad on the phone or tell her sister to call, but the encouraging calls that eased her solitude had basically stopped.

Janet was disappointed when the coming of calls slowed, and thoughts of abandonment once again emerged to the forefront of her consciousness.

*What did I expect? For them to call every day for a year while Marcus was gone?* she thought to herself while chewing a bite of cold steak. Of course she hadn't, yet Janet knew she could pick up the phone and call any of her family members if she needed to, night or day, because whatever happened in life, her family would always be there for her. The love and devotion found in family was designed by God as a support system, and family helped family no matter what; friends, as Janet had unfortunately discovered, not so much.

She pushed the steamed broccoli around on her plate with the fork. Neither the broccoli nor the medium-rare sirloin remained even mildly warm, but that was no matter. The food had little flavor, anyway.

The young woman at the next table giggled provocatively at some corny joke her partner had whispered. Janet couldn't remember the last time she had giggled like that. In fact, she couldn't remember the last time she had giggled at all. Her brow wrinkled as she concentrated, thinking back to the tense last two weeks before deployment began. Marcus had stopped even trying to lighten her spirits like he usually would do. They'd said goodbye to their normal routine and normal conversations long before he'd left.

No messages.

So often lately Janet caught herself holding that phone like it was her only lifeline, which, in a way, it was. That device was often her only source of connection to any semblance of a relationship. If every relationship were as close as she was to that phone or every partner as dedicated or dependent, the divorce rate wouldn't be nearly as high.

*What would I do without that blasted phone?* Janet pondered as she chewed another bite.

As if on cue, the phone on the pub-height table began to vibrate. She expectantly reached for it and quickly pushed the button "View Now" to read the text message. The tingle of butterflies in her belly happened most times the phone rang, anxious to hear from him, yet concerned the conversation wouldn't end well.

Her anticipatory smile turned into a scoff as she read the text. It was just some ridiculous mass chain message from one of the other nurses at work. As what her dad liked to say, if she had a nickel for every time she'd gotten her hopes up only to be let down, she'd have a lot of nickels by now.

She finished her steak and flagged down her waiter to order dessert. She deserved to indulge herself in a rich fudge brownie paired with vanilla bean ice cream and hot fudge sauce.

"Ah, yes!" Janet sighed dreamily when the waiter returned minutes later with her bowl.

"Is that for me?" a voice behind her asked.

Janet turned to see Russ standing behind her chair and smiled.

"You'll have to get your own!" she laughed. "This one is mine!" She pulled her bowl closer to her in a joking gesture.

"Mind if I join you?" Russ asked.

Janet motioned with her spoon to all of the empty chairs at the table and said, "Take your pick if you want. Are you here alone?"

"I'm just coming to meet some guys from work," he waved over in the direction of a table of men all dressed just like he was in button ups, slacks, and expensive shoes. Janet noted the way the shirt stretched across his broad chest.

"So surely your date didn't stand you up again…" the handsome man pried with a devilish grin. Janet sucked in a breath thinking of the last time they'd met like this, and her body tingled the same way it had that night when his hand grazed her back while leading her to the cab.

Over the last couple months, he had crossed her path quite often at the nursing home. Every time he came to see his mom, Russ made a point to stop by the nurse's station to say hello. The other nurses had always stared with googly eyes whenever Russ came to visit, but now that he came by to speak to them, the ladies couldn't get enough of his baby blues.

"Actually, my date is half a world away," she replied sadly while stirring her ice cream.

Russ looked confused so Janet held out her left hand to show him her ring. "He's deployed," she added.

Nodding in understanding, Russ smiled half-heartedly, "All the good ones are married."

Janet shrugged.

"So how long has he been gone?" Russ asked.

"Remember that night at the airport?" Janet said, and he nodded. "Well, he'd just gotten on the plane."

"Ah, I knew something was wrong with you, but I didn't want to pry." He flagged down the waiter and asked for a menu.

"I wish that was all that was wrong," Janet mumbled.

Russ thanked the waiter who sat the cold drink down in front of him, then looked at Janet with a confused expression. "What do you mean?"

"Well, let's see. First, he announced that he didn't want kids after we had be trying for two years. Then, he *volunteers* to deploy. I mean, it wasn't like our marriage was great, but how miserable was he to rather be in a war zone than with me?" Janet shook her head, regretting saying those words out loud to someone else. "Ugh, let's change the subject."

Russ didn't miss a beat as he began talking about the weather predictions for the week, and she smiled, thankful that he was courteous enough to change the subject. Janet had forgotten how it felt to enjoy a conversation with a man.

It felt secure. She felt safe.

The exact opposite of the feelings of abandonment she'd been battling.

# Chapter 5

The scorching sun beamed down as he squinted and brushed away another drop of sweat from his sopping forehead. He'd already taken a shower that day but longed desperately for another as the dust stirred with every brisk step he took closer to his barracks. If he hurried, he would have time to call her before she went to work that morning and still have time to shower again before the chow hall started serving supper.

The nine-hour time difference made communication difficult. When he was getting up each morning, she was going to bed. When he was free in the evenings, she was at work. When she was free after work, he was sleeping. He was simply grateful for each moment he was able to hear her voice, although her voice often seemed distracted rather than doting.

He understood that his absence left her frustrated at times, like when she attended church barbecues solo on drill weekends or a friend's wedding by herself because he didn't want to put on a tie on a Saturday. He knew she was having trouble coping with being alone and doing all of those things by herself this year, but he wished her voice would sound happier on the phone. The dejection he detected brought with it a wave of guilt.

Marcus knew she blamed him for this deployment.

But what he couldn't understand was how she could be so blinded by her own sacrifices that she couldn't be proud of him for his. The disparity of their feelings often led to a lot of tension when they did finally have time to talk on the phone after he left.

*Maybe today won't be like that*, he hoped. Maybe today she'd be excited to hear from him. Maybe today she'd go on and on about how much she loved him like she used to do rather than the silence she'd adopted over the last few months. Maybe he could sense the beautiful smile in her voice instead of envisioning the wide-eyed way she had looked at him that day in the kitchen. Maybe, just maybe, they would make it through a whole conversation without him feeling like dirt for hurting her.

Nearing the door to the barracks, Marcus quickened his pace as the wind picked up and began swirling the powdery dust around him like a cloud of early morning fog, only this fog was made of dirt, not moisture. He missed those early morning fogs back home when he'd get up before daylight to drink a cup of coffee and listen to the sounds of the world waking up. Their little cul-de-sac was close enough to the center of town that he could hear the honking of cars on their morning commute but far enough away from the traffic that the horns didn't drown out the birds chirping. He felt closer to God during those dawning moments than any other time throughout the day, but that closeness was harder to find in the desert.

Even the memory of the view from his back porch—the tall oak tree, the wooden swing, the green grass—Marcus wished he had taken more pictures before he left home, but there had been so many other things going on, so many other things to square away. He hadn't wanted to leave her with so much to do because he didn't want to add any responsibility or stress to her life when he could avoid it. He didn't want her to feel strained this whole year doing the things he should have been doing.

Janet was amazed at how old the lady in the mirror looked this morning. As she brushed the pink toothbrush back and forth across her teeth, she stared blindly at the ornate silver frame around the mirror and wondered how long before her light brown hair started to match it in color. The bags under her eyes appeared a deeper, darker blue than usual, much too dark for any concealer to hide. Whether or not the concealer would work, she'd at least make the effort to avoid the questioning, sympathetic glances. She detested those looks people gave her and could hear their thoughts: *Poor girl all by herself must not be sleeping well, How sad that her husband is away, Poor thing must have cried herself to sleep.*

*Ugh,* she thought.

Janet regretted how pessimistic this deployment had made her feel about everything, about people, about love, about happiness, about everything, including the face staring back at her in the mirror. Women her age weren't supposed to have such pronounced forehead wrinkles, but she guessed that was her cross to bear for squinting her eyebrows in frustration multiple times throughout each day. *Stupid wrinkles,* she was thinking as she rinsed the pink toothbrush and placed it back in its silver holder when her thoughts were interrupted by the ringing cell phone lying on the edge of the king-sized bed a few feet from the other side of the door.

She walked barefoot across the mingled brown carpet, which desperately needed to be ripped up and replaced with something made this decade, to the bed and picked up the phone from the white down comforter she and Marcus had picked out together when they'd upgraded to a king-sized bed not long after he'd returned from his first deployment. That had been a good shopping trip, back in the days when they still agreed on everything, flopping down on bed after bed like Goldilocks until they both announced simultaneously, "This is it!" then burst into laughter at their synchronized outbursts.

With neither of them being aware of the changes, that blissful honeymoon phase had ended before he got the notice they had both dreaded since he had signed the reenlistment papers this last time. She hadn't noticed the first morning he didn't kiss her goodbye when he left for work or the first night they sat at opposite ends of the sofa instead of cuddling while watching a movie. When she finally did realize the change, she could not recall how long they'd been off track, and it seemed too late to go back.

"Hello," she abruptly answered on the third ring.

"Good morning, beautiful," Marcus's voice came through the phone in response to her brisk hello. He smiled as he spoke, hoping she would sense his expression through the receiver.

"Hey, how are you?" Janet sighed with mixed relief that he'd finally called and a tinge of remorse that her life now revolved around waiting for this kind of calls.

"Good, just been a long week. Sorry I haven't been able to call," he said disappointingly. She didn't sound like she was in a bad mood, so that was good.

"It's fine," she assured, but he knew that it wasn't. "I really can't talk long now. I've got a long day ahead, a twelve hour shift, and I'm already running behind because I didn't sleep well."

Marcus understood not sleeping well. He'd gone from a pillow-top, king-sized mattress to a twin mattress that felt more like a sheet of plywood than a bed. The all-night missions and occasional rockets exploding near the base didn't help matters any further. He knew her problems weren't worse than nearby explosions, but he wouldn't dare tell her that for fear she'd be the one to blow up. If he could still be content and, at least, feign happiness thousands of miles away from everything he loved, why couldn't she sound glad to hear from him?

"Why are you having trouble sleeping?" he empathized.

"I don't know, just am," she sighed, wondering the same thing herself. *Why does it matter to him that I'm not sleeping? If he cared about how I slept, he shouldn't have gone halfway across the world and given me reasons for sleepless nights,* she thought.

Janet had tried so hard to not be angry toward him, and for several months she had managed to keep at bay her resentment of his blatant disregard for their future and her hopes of becoming a mother. He'd taken away something she desperately wanted, then left her there alone to cope with the loss.

"So how long before your next mission?" she asked to change the subject.

He knew that was her way of saying, "How long till you go several days without calling me again?" like he could control being sent out on missions. He ignored the bitter tone of her voice and simply said he didn't know, but he thought he had a few days off between missions, and the next couple trips should only take one day each, not overnighters like this last one.

"Did your mission go well?" she tentatively questioned. Janet had learned during the first deployment to not ask explicitly about his missions, not even *Is everyone okay?* because he wasn't allowed to answer. Even after he'd gotten home the first time, he'd never shared with her his experiences on missions. The most she'd ever gotten in details was about the mission during which a soldier in his unit was killed by an explosion, and she'd learned very little about that situation, just that Marcus had seen it happen.

"Of course," he responded. "You know how awesome I am!" he tried to tease.

Janet didn't think his joke was funny, which was ironic considering his sense of humor was what had attracted her to Marcus in the very beginning.

Conversation stalled, and the static of the international call moved into the forefront as they both tried to think of something to talk about. Like usual, they each told about menial things like a cute E-card she'd seen online, what crafts she'd found on Pinterest, what happened while Marcus was at the gym, what they both had eaten for lunch, who said what on Facebook—insignificant facets of day-to-day life to which they clung—but topics were soon exhausted, and they grew silent. Sometimes Janet wondered what they had talked about before the deployment and mused if this was it, if all they ever discussed were the events—or the lack of them—of the day.

"I love you," Marcus said quietly, interrupting her commiserating thoughts. His voice sounded weak and fearful, very unlike the strong, outspoken man she remembered who would not hesitate to assert his opinions when they argued over the years. Early in their marriage, they overlooked or even laughed about disagreements; but with time, they each developed the desire to be the one who was right in the end. Marcus had usually won whether he was right or not because Janet eventually got tired of arguing and would give up, but since the reenlistment, they seldom argued at all.

The further they drifted apart, the more *who* was right seemed more important than *what* was right to Marcus, so Janet had given up trying to correct him when she knew he was on the wrong track. Letting him win was easier then, but even his tone of voice had changed drastically since he had been deployed. She was not sure where the difference originated, and she was hesitant to probe to find out.

"I love you, too," she replied, sounding much more preoccupied than she had intended. Janet didn't mean for her voice to sound so distant—she really did love him desperately—but her frustrations often reflected in her voice, which is how he had usually known when some underlying problem was bothering her. Her face could easily be read, which is the reason she almost refused to video chat since his deployment; that, plus seeing him made her ache somewhere deep inside, remembering how good life used to be before he had given up on their dreams and she had subsequently given up on their future.

Marcus's sentiments were different. Seeing her even briefly through a computer screen made him remember what he was fighting to come home to. It broke his heart that she did not want to video chat, that she did not want to see his face, the face that had lain on the pillow next to hers for almost a decade now. Aware that she had been unhappy with their relationship for some time now, he understood her feelings to some extent but still didn't like the result. One weak decision had transformed him from her partner to someone he couldn't identify.

Every night when he lay down on his rigid mattress, he thought about lying in the plush king-sized bed next to her back home. He smiled as he recalled the way she would wiggle and root him nearly off the bed some nights, then argue that he was the bed hog. He smiled at the memory of lazy Sunday mornings they slept in before cooking breakfast together as she hummed "Oh, How I Love Jesus" while flipping pancakes.

"I wish I was at home," Marcus said.

Janet didn't know how to respond. She wanted him to be home, too, but she had a hard time expressing her feelings since he'd hurt her so much. She wasn't still angry, but she wasn't over it either, yet he sounded so pitiful, and the aching in his voice was hard for Janet to acknowledge.

Saying their goodbyes before she rushed off to work—last day before the weekend—the distance between the couple echoed in the silence, an expanse neither knew how to bridge.

# Chapter 6

Janet turned the key in the ignition, listening to the sound of the engine as it started to warm up. Putting the car into reverse, she took a sip of her hazelnut-flavored iced coffee, wishing just this once that she could handle a dose of caffeine rather than this decaf imposter. She'd gone off caffeine months ago because falling asleep at night was difficult enough without the extra buzz from coffee and sodas keeping her awake.

She disliked getting up this early most mornings, but some mornings weren't that bad. She was most productive in the mornings, truth be told—getting laundry and dishes done. Coming home from work knowing there were no dirty dishes in the sink was a pretty awesome feeling. However, finding motivation to keep a clean house was difficult when one lived alone.

Thinking of the phone conversation they'd just finished, Janet's mind wandered off during her quiet drive to work. That drive used to be Janet's favorite time of the day, the time she would spend talking to God about her thankfulness and her concerns, but now this drive to the nursing home constituted her most uncomfortable twenty minutes of the daily one thousand four hundred forty. She cranked up the radio to the local oldies station to keep from rehashing that morning's bland phone conversation with Marcus and to drown out the restless dreams of carefully folded flags and twenty-one gun salutes from the night before, hoping to keep them from interrupting her day.

After a brief interlude with Elvis, the Temptations, and Bob Dylan, Janet parked her car in the rear lot and headed through the heavy metal door to start her day's work. With her purse hung inside her metal locker in the nurse's lounge, Janet's morning routine was underway. After checking the charts and doing her morning paperwork, Janet walked down the hall to greet her first patient of the day who uncomplainingly waited for the hot breakfast Janet had just retrieved from the ladies in the bland cafeteria that hadn't been renovated or redecorated since the 1980s.

The butterless grits jiggled as Janet sat the plastic tray on the bedside table.

"Good morning, Mrs. Tanner," Janet greeted the eighty-two-year-old white-haired woman sitting in the recliner by the closed window. Janet unwrapped the straw and placed it in the carton. "I brought your juice."

Mrs. Tanner smiled and continued looking out the window at the flowers. Despite sometimes not knowing her own name, Lucille always wore a smile.

Every morning after dressing, Lucille Tanner would sit in that navy chair staring out at the courtyard garden, her eyes seemingly captivated by the magnetic pull of the rose bushes. Janet's eyes followed Mrs. Tanner's gaze to the full crimson blooms and wished something as simple as rose bushes could make her smile, too. She recalled sitting on the steps of her mother's porch admiring the beautiful rainbow of impatiens all over the front yard and watching her niece sniff a gerbera daisy so hard that the petals would fall limply to the ground.

She wheeled the bedside table closer to the older woman and nestled it between the tattered recliner and the smudged window. The cleaning crew had been short-staffed for months now, and the patients' rooms were starting to reflect the inattention. Janet made a mental note to bring some glass cleaner with her tomorrow to give the window a good swipe to enhance Lucille's view of her one delight in this drab backdrop—the flower garden.

"G'mornin," Lucille greeted in her quivering Southern drawl, turning slowly to face the young nurse. Her smile faltered a bit, briefly revealing the confusion she battled endlessly.

Alzheimer's was a terrifying disease to Janet. She prayed every day that it would never happen to her or her family. Her great-grandmother had suffered from it, although Janet remembered little to none of her namesake's struggles because Janet had been very young when the woman had died. Daily working with dementia sufferers who forgot even the simplest things wrenched Janet's heart, and she felt the pain her mother and grandmother must have endured from watching her great-grandmother wither away.

Often, a patient would call Janet by the name of one of his or her children, siblings, or friends, and she answered to whatever names they called her: Marie, April, Kevin, Shad. The name she was called mattered little compared to the people she was helping. For a brief moment, acting like she was someone's sister, or even someone's son, was worth it if only to keep that look of confusion off the tired faces of her patients.

"The roses sure are pretty today, aren't they, Mrs. Tanner?" Janet remarked as she contemplated the older woman's fascination with the flowers. As she, too, looked at the garden, Janet realized the double roses appeared triple in the morning sun, even through the grimy glass; the assorted red, pink, and yellow knockout bushes were so full of blooms it was a wonder the stems didn't break.

"Yes, dear, they are. Tom plants them for me, you know. He planted them in the front yard of our old house when the kids were small, but those died one cold winter back in the '80s. Do you remember that?" she asked weakly, looking expectantly up at Janet. The glazed look in her eyes warned Janet that today would be one of the tough ones. On bad days, the sweet little old lady staring at the roses could become borderline aggressive.

"Was that the winter it snowed so much?" Janet pried the old woman's memory even though she herself had been just a small child in the 1980s and remembered absolutely nothing about the weather in those years.

Without acknowledging Janet's question, Lucille said, "I told him to put pine straw around them before it got so cold, but he never listens to me." Lucille complained of her husband's lack of attentiveness. "I would'a done it myself, but I had my hands full planning the children's play at church."

Little did Mrs. Tanner realize how thoughtful her husband was, especially compared to many other spouses of dementia patients Janet had seen. Lucille was one of the lucky ones with a large, tightly-knit family who cared about not only her daily needs, but also her happiness and comfort. Janet had some patients who never received a single visitor, some whose children lived across the country and some whose family couldn't bear to witness the mental state of their loved one.

Lucille's husband was a faithful visitor despite her worsening condition. Usually, she recognized him, although often in her mind they were still a young married couple with children running barefoot around the grassy backyard. Her memory seemed to be stuck in that timeframe: football practices, PTA meetings, bake sales, and all. Janet remembered the previous Christmas when Lucille had kept talking about the shiny red bicycle with chrome handlebars that Johnny was getting from Santa and the pink lacey dresses she was busy sewing for the girls.

Janet would love to have seen Lucille's sewing handiwork. She had heard the Tanners mention their mother's hobby on several occasions, how she used to stitch most of their clothes when they were young and how she could find a crafty use of things most people would consider junk.

Even with the current obsession with repurposing items with projects found on Pinterest, Janet could not imagine what use anyone could find for jars of acorns, rocks, and sandspurs they said Lucille kept in the chifforobe in her sewing room, although she could easily picture the petite lady in the recliner concentrating as she cross-stitched roses onto a pillow case. Her wrinkled hands shook too badly now to thread the eye of a tiny sewing needle, but she still sporadically picked up her crochet hooks and sat them in her lap while she watched *The Price is Right* or *The Bold and the Beautiful.*

As Janet turned to leave Mrs. Tanner's private room, the small vanity mirror above the undersized sink caught her eye. She turned away quickly without really looking at herself, but the brief glimpse was enough to give Janet the sudden urge to stick her tongue out at her own reflection like a five-year-old. As she closed the door to Mrs. Tanner's room, Janet paused a moment to stare at the old woman sitting in the chair still looking out the window and felt an ache as she remembered the first long-term care patient she'd treated years ago.

Janet had become very close to the woman in a short span of time, and she had felt robbed when the lady only lived a couple weeks after coming to stay at Springing Hills. The doctors had discovered the first cancerous cells, and the woman's health had deteriorated more quickly than Janet had ever seen; although her spirit remained upbeat. She'd been brought to the nursing home to recover from surgery they thought would remove most of the cancer, but it obviously didn't work.

Relief and joy had spread through Janet when she had seen people clearing out Mrs. Latimore's room that day years before, until one of the nurses informed her that Mrs. Latimore had gone home to be with Jesus rather than home with her family. Janet's heart had broken, and she'd barely made it to her break before breaking down in tears. The woman had seemed so lively and so hopeful of "kickin" cancer's butt," as she'd confidently told the young nurse every day.

She'd felt Mrs. Latimore had been cheated by dying less than a month after discovering she was sick, stripped of precious time she should have been spending with grandkids, but in view of the old lady now sitting sadly day after day by the window, Janet understood the blessing of a quick passing rather than witnessing a patient deteriorating for months or even years.

After closing the door to Mrs. Tanner's room, Janet hurried into the hallway to visit the next patient on her morning rounds, reflecting on the haggard face that had stared back at her in the mirror at home earlier that morning, barely resembling the young nurse who'd driven home in tears the day Mrs. Latimore died. A lot had changed since then.

Janet had always been her own worst critic according to Marcus, and she knew that he was right. It had taken a long time for her to accept the extra ten pounds she'd gained since college, and she wasn't sure if she'd *ever* accept going up a pants size, although she had learned to live with it. The scrubs were so unflattering that she tried to convince herself no one could look gorgeous in them anyway.

Those extra pounds seemed to have appeared overnight, and Janet would never understand how a woman's weight could so quickly go up and wouldn't go down more than two pounds no matter how many miles she walked on the treadmill or how many hamburgers and French fries she had foregone. Janet actually couldn't remember the last time she ordered fries—she had been opting for a side salad since fast food restaurants all started providing that option—but her pants were still tight around her waist and thighs.

Janet wondered if her extra weight had changed how Marcus looked at her or if he even looked at her at all anymore. Early in their relationship, Marcus told her how beautiful she was on a regular basis, but he had seemed to stop noticing her in the last couple years.

One time, Janet had broken down and bought a lace set of lingerie that was so risqué she had grabbed a flannel nightgown from the adjacent rack just to throw over it in her shopping cart, so no one would see the skimpy red teddy. After tousling her hair to get the sexy unkempt look when she adorned the nighty to bed later that night, Marcus had flipped off the bedside lamp as soon as she walked in the room, then rolled away with his back toward her and started snoring.

She didn't know whether or not he'd even seen her outfit before he turned out the light—she told herself that he hadn't, but part of Janet believed he simply wasn't interested in what she was offering—and Janet felt more insecure than ever before as a result of his inattentiveness.

Yet this was the path she had chosen wholeheartedly and pledged before God to keep until death. Her cup, which had runneth over a few years ago, had not gone dry—she recognized her blessings of a warm home and secure job—but her cup was definitely not full anymore. Too many areas of her life were lacking fulfillment.

Janet had poured so much hope into starting a family and so many prayers into her marriage but to seemingly no avail. She often felt as though her faith was running out. She trusted that God would fill her cup again in his own time, but patience was a virtue she lacked, and his clock was ticking too slowly for her liking.

The time clock at work was ticking leisurely by, as well, her Friday dragging its feet keeping her from the weekend. When

Marcus had been home, she would bounce out the door at 3:01 every Friday afternoon when her shift ended to hurry home, change into something nicer than scrubs, and get dinner started before he got home a couple hours later.

With no one waiting at home to eat dinner with, Janet no longer bounced out the backdoor every afternoon, but she met the work day's end happily just the same. Hours going from room to room, one sick or dying patient after another, trying to both meet their needs and lift their spirits, Janet's energy was zapped by quitting time, and she had little strength left to bear her own loads.

Sometimes, the emotional burden of their lonely gazes through windows and sad conversations about the family members who rarely visited left Janet drained and longing for the twelve-hour night shift when the patients should be sleeping. Even with the nightmares and midnight changing of soiled sheets, nights were fairly easy to handle.

Janet would take any shift except late afternoons. Early in her long-term care nursing career, she had worked the sundowner shift for almost a year before requesting a shift change. Seeing the sweet little old ladies throw their supper to the tile floor or swing a cane at her as though she were a robber breaking into their house was too much for Janet to do day after day. Mornings were much better. Most of the dementia patients were alert in the mornings, but the violent tendencies of the disease took hold as their memories slipped with the day's progression.

The selfish feelings of wishing she could sometimes meet their needs without building relationships snuck into her day on occasion, but Janet knew that chatting with her was the most interaction some of these people would have all day, so she did it gladly. She listened when they felt well enough to tell stories of growing up during the war, and she, in turn, told them stories of her own—even if she had to make something up—when she sensed they needed a laugh.

As emotionally trying as watching another human being suffer might be, showing each one that he or she was important was more rewarding than whatever hurt Janet experienced. Too many people wanted to shut a door, to block out what gave them pain without realizing the preciousness of each experience they were shutting out, which is how so many of Janet's patients came to be so lonely. Their families couldn't bear to watch them deteriorate day after day, so they secured their loved ones away like shutting the lid on the casket before walking away in tears. Many never came back to visit even once, reassuring themselves that Momma or Daddy would not recognize them anyhow.

Their loneliness had worn off on her during this deployment, as though she carried it home with her every day, herself becoming the patient locked away while everyone else's lives went on without her.

"I lift my hands to you in prayer. I thirst for you as parched land thirsts for rain," Marcus read quietly so as not to wake his roommate who'd just returned from a long mission and desperately needed the rest. While the tired man sharing his room slept soundly, Marcus had restlessly tossed and turned until he'd finally given up and started reading his Bible. If he were going to be awake, he might as well get something positive out of his insomnia, so Marcus had flipped straight to the center of his Bible, began turning the pages of Psalms, then stopped at Psalm 143.

Marcus empathized with David's isolation and experienced his own yearning for deliverance. Though he wasn't being cornered by enemies out to kill him like David had been when he wrote this cry to God, Marcus was at war thousands of miles away from the land he loved, separated from the people he cared about, his home.

Both remembering a time of fellowship with God, the two men, who lived centuries apart, knew well the desire to have that closeness again and the struggle to fill the ever-present void that grows from separation between God and his children.

Marcus's bunkmate had asked him once not long after they had arrived overseas why he spent so much time reading his Bible, and Marcus had simply made light of the action, saying he didn't have anything else to read. His friend had laughed, and that had been the end of the discussion. After his offhand comment, though, Marcus felt ashamed that he hadn't given his friend a true answer and realized that his callous attitude toward worship and studying his Bible hadn't developed overnight.

For several years, Marcus's Bible study had consisted of what he heard at church, and his fellowship with God entailed saying the blessing before family meals. That was it. He had not invested time into the relationship, and the security he had once felt had unraveled.

Marcus had previously attributed his lack of desire to talk to God to his unhappy situation at home. For a long time, he had prayed multiple times a day, and those conversations with God had almost always ended with Marcus asking God for a child; not in the way a six-year-old prays for a puppy, but in the way a faithful servant petitions God for the desires of his heart. "Don't worry about anything, and with prayers of thanksgiving, make your requests known to God," Marcus's mother had taught him early.

Yet he couldn't help worrying after seeing his wife give herself hormone injections night after night and then seeing the disappointment spread over her face every time the test showed one blue line instead of two. Eventually, he had stopped asking God for a baby, and it wasn't long after that he had stopped asking God for anything at all.

Marcus wasn't sure where the cycle began and ended, kind of like the chicken and egg dilemma. Whether his strained relationship with God began before or after his relationship with his wife became tense, Marcus was unsure. He only knew that he wanted to get away from the pressure of his situation and was almost relieved when he received the chance to deploy.

Now, while looking back at his actions and attitude, his guilt-ridden conscience chastised him daily for forsaking his God-appointed responsibility of being the spiritual leader of his household.

Looking at men of the world who didn't take their leadership role seriously and instead left their wives the challenge of teaching their children right from wrong or lorded their "head of household" title over their wives commanding obedience, Marcus had vowed to be better than that when he proposed to Janet, but he had failed to uphold that promise. He had not supported Janet and hadn't been her strength when she was most vulnerable. Instead, he had turned his back on their situation because avoiding her was easier than faithfully pressing on toward a goal he doubted would ever be fulfilled. He had not trusted God enough to keep going forward, so he had taken an easier path.

"Let me hear of your unfailing love each morning, for I am trusting you. Show me where to walk, for I give myself to you," he whispered as he read on.

Like David's spirit all those centuries ago, Marcus's was growing faint; his heart, dismayed. Similar to the dry desert where he'd been stationed these last several months, Marcus felt parched for God. The Living Water was harder to find in the desert, he believed. Without regular doses of Sunday School, worship service, prayer meetings—the things he'd often done out of mere obligation before and those strengthening reinforcements each week—Marcus was now lacking the support and guidance he had once felt in his spiritual life.

He'd known from his previous deployment that he wouldn't be able to attend many church services on base. Although the military chaplains led both Catholic and Protestant services each week, Marcus was usually resting to go on a mission, after returning from a mission, or actually out on a mission when the services took place. Even when he did occasionally go, he didn't feel the Spirit moving in that watered-down service.

Each service was different depending on the denomination of the chaplain. Sometimes they sang either with or without music, whatever the chaplain chose, and sometimes they didn't sing at all. Marcus missed singing the old hymns from the Southern Baptist Hymnal in his country church back home.

He would love to hear his grandma sing "Keep on the Firing Line" or himself belt out a triumphant "Victory in Jesus," although he hadn't felt much victory lately. He missed worshipping in that little church surrounded by people he loved, and Marcus wished he had realized at the time how fortunate he was to simply have the freedom to be there each Sunday morning singing those hymns.

Pouring sweat through the 120-degree days and sleeping in a toboggan hat and wool socks at night in the desert—he would never be able to comprehend why he was cold in the 80-degree weather—Marcus felt silly for ever complaining of something so minuscule as the temperature in the church sanctuary.

Out in the desert, he experienced more loneliness than he had expected, and it wasn't caused by distance from his family. Marcus's deepest loneliness was from the distance he sensed between him and God. While it was easy to feel God's love from the comfort of the church pew back home, it was hard to hold on to in the midst of a war.

"Teach me to do your will, for you are my God. May your gracious Spirit lead me forward on a firm footing," he read on in verse eight. *Man, the Spirit is really dealing with me tonight*, Marcus contemplated, feeling a deep connection to the psalmist. When he had enlisted this last time, the inevitability of deployment was made known to him by his superior officers, but he had put his life completely in the Army's hands the day he signed that reenlistment paperwork.

While he had found many reasons to justify his actions, some nights now he wondered if he had done the right thing. His marriage was crumbling, and he didn't know how to hold it together. Sometimes, Marcus even questioned God's plan for their future. With a lot of time on his hands to think about his poor decisions and how they had injured his relationships, Marcus knew he needed to put his priorities in order, but he worried how his new priorities would fit into life back home.

Yet every day when he left his barracks, Marcus stepped out with faith that God had a purpose for his life and trusted that God would protect him through whatever that purpose entailed. Surely this deployment wouldn't be the end of their life together, surely God wouldn't reward his service to his country by allowing him to lose the one person who mattered most in his life. Certainly God wouldn't reward his sacrifices by tearing apart his family and home.

"For the glory of your name, O Lord, preserve my life," he read. "Because of your faithfulness, bring me out of this distress." Marcus prayed for God to preserve his *whole* life, not to just keep him alive. Life was so much more than simply breathing in and out each day, and he was beginning to realize that he didn't want to go home to a life without her in it. For now, though, he'd just imagine his grandma's voice urging him to "Keep on the Firing Line" and do just that.

# Chapter 7

She got home from work Friday evening and sat on the swing before going in.

A warm tingle flowed through her veins as she recalled the stranger's hand on her back. That small touch seemed to have unlocked something within her; it made her long for happiness again, made her no longer want to settle for less.

She used to have more. Through glossy eyes, she stared at the heart Marcus had carved into their tree the day they'd signed the purchasing papers at the real estate office. A small smile formed as she recalled how she'd had to use the same knife with which he'd carved "Marcus loves Janet 4 ever" to dig a splinter out of his hand later that evening. One would've thought the poor fellow was dying from the way he whined about that little splinter.

Now, he, the same guy who whined over a splinter, was at war. How men could be so strong towards adversity, yet so weak over little things like splinters and spiders would always bewilder Janet. Anyone who could have witnessed the way Marcus had come unglued on their sixth anniversary trip to the lake and nearly tipped their paddle boat trying to get away from a spider would never picture him as a soldier. The episode of Janet picking up his ball cap from the floor of the boat where it had fallen when he'd jumped out of his seat slapping the spider into the water had turned into a running joke.

She shook her head as though the memories were drawn on an etch-a-sketch and could be erased by a mere rattle of the board. *If only it were that simple*, she thought.

With eyes turned toward Heaven, Janet wondered if Marcus was looking at the same stars she was looking at, like the couples in the sappy love stories always did. She imagined Marcus as the Hollywood hero—a rugged cowboy from an old western, belt buckles, spurs, the whole lot—gazing at the brightest star in the desert sky (at least, the desert aspect of her daydream was real), whispering her name softly by the campfire, followed by the words "I miss you." As Janet closed her eyes, she listened hard with her heart, trying to sense Marcus even though she knew it was a silly notion.

She opened her eyes. Her practical and realistic-to-a-fault attitude promptly halted her daydream with *Duh, it's morning over there!* The brisk reminder of the vast distance between them and the reality that he could never be gazing at the same stars she was gazing at interrupted her solemn mood and snapped her resolve firmly back into place. Sniffling one last time and blinking her blue eyes resolutely, Janet swung her bare feet down, planting them firmly on the dry grass.

She knew better than to think about it as she picked up her purse from the grass and stood to walk toward the empty house. Her aching heart knew better than to dream, but she often felt like one of the moths that are being drawn to the light. She couldn't help herself sometimes, but life was no dream; she often wished deployment was just a nightmare from which she'd soon wake up.

With keys in one hand and purse in the other, Janet unlocked the sliding glass door on the back porch and stepped inside the desolate den adjacent to the dining room. She softly closed the door as though she were a teenager silently slipping in two hours after curfew on a school night, praying with each tip toe not to wake her parents sleeping down the hall. As she did this, she was also vaguely recalling their first night in their new home when she and Marcus had been anything but quiet.

Janet's reactions of coming home to an empty house varied. Times like tonight, she was excessively quiet. Other times, she was so paranoid that she would overtly make a lot of noise—rattling the keys, slamming the door, shuffling her shoes on the tile floor—all so the "robber" inside would hear her and would sneak out through another door and not be caught in the act.

*Paranoia thrown into overdrive for certain*, she thought.

Janet attributed that erratic wary feeling to her nerves, which were stretched more than an Olympic gymnast does when getting ready for a meet. Continuing to tiptoe through the hallway without flipping on a single light switch, Janet imagined herself ten years younger as the strong-willed woman who had lived alone working her way through college without the slightest insecurity, the woman who had gone home to her tiny apartment solo at midnight without the smallest worry.

Trying to recall her younger self made Janet appallingly glum. When she was flitting around as an optimistic twenty-year-old, had she been warned what she'd be like now, she would have laughed. She could hardly believe how her attitude and outlook had been changed by life—from tough to fragile, independent to needy, alone to lonely, cheerful to…well, whatever she was now. The woman who worked three jobs to make ends meet and still had energy to stay up late on her nights off was now exhausted before she even got off work from her only job and was already in bed by nine.

Unsure when the change had taken place, Janet often speculated how she had become this woman she didn't even recognize. Standing in their master bedroom, she undressed letting the scrubs drop to the floor where it would lay several days until she finally decided to do the laundry. Until Marcus had deployed this second time, she had never realized how long she could go without doing the laundry. Janet had enough clothes that she could easily go for an entire week without washing any of them, two weeks depending on how many shifts she worked.

Standing in the dark of the spacious master bathroom wearing only her lavender panties with tiny white polka dots and basic nude bra—so unlike the newlywed days when she thought all undergarments should be a seductively matched set—Janet removed her earrings one by one, slid the backs into place before setting the pair of dainty silver hoops in the small white ceramic bowl sitting on the counter by the sink and ran her fingers across the pink rosebuds circling the rim just as she did every night while getting ready for bed.

She didn't have to turn down the sheets. They were still tossed back just as she'd left them when she woke that morning. Lying down and wrapping herself in the covers, Janet's eyes closed, but the loneliness had set in so rest would not come.

Saying she was lonely sounded like an excuse to blame Marcus for the turmoil she felt, and Janet knew that what was going on in her core was not entirely his fault. Just like most nights, she lay awake for what seemed like hours, eyes closed, trying to block everything out of her mind so her body could relax.

Tonight, the thoughts keeping her awake weren't the usual depressed musings of loneliness. Tonight, every time she closed her eyes, Janet could feel the exploring gaze of the man at the restaurant. She tried desperately not to imagine his body as hers quivered at the thoughts she shouldn't be having, but she couldn't fight her mind. She squeezed her eyelids shut, willing the images to go away, and shook her head violently when they remained.

Janet tried picturing a map of the United States and naming the states and their capitals. She tried counting to one hundred, and she even tried to list the books of the Bible backwards. Still, she couldn't get him out of her thoughts.

"Ugh!" She exhaled with aggravation.

Tossing back the sheets and swinging her legs over the side of bed, Janet hardly stood before her knees dropped straight to the floor and her folded hands rested where she had just been lying. She squeezed her eyes shut hard, but a single tear of frustration escaped and rolled down her cheek.

With chest rising and falling over and over again while she knelt in silence, she couldn't find the words to express her turmoil to God. She bit her bottom lip to stop it from quivering, unsure how to express herself in her own words, and began repeating a prayer she'd heard all her life.

"God," Janet whispered shakily, "grant me the serenity to accept the things I cannot change because, Lord, you know I can't make him come home today or change what we've been through the last few years. Grant me the courage to change the things I can, like my attitude, God. Help me change my attitude, give me the courage to be happy when I really want to be sad because I'm tired of fake smiling. Help me to stop feeling so lonely. And God"—she paused, swallowing hard and opening her eyes toward the ceiling—"grant me the wisdom to know the difference, the wisdom to do the right thing when everything seems wrong. Amen."

Janet wiped the tear from her cheek as she climbed back into bed, wrapped herself tightly in the comforter and snuggled to Marcus's pillow until she fell asleep.

## Chapter 8

For most Saturday mornings, Janet lay around lazily soaking up all the free time and staying in her pajamas until noon or later, but not today. She'd gotten up early like she was going to work, gotten dressed in cut-off shorts and a breathable t-shirt, then cooked herself some pancakes. No more sitting around feeling sorry for herself, Janet had determined.

She was just sitting down at the corner bench in her eat-in kitchen when the doorbell rang.

Startled, she felt her stomach drop and immediately thought the worst. Who would ring her doorbell at this time of the morning and why? That ever-present panic she'd been suppressing for months started to quiver to the surface. She hesitantly walked to the door and was met by a pleasant surprise.

"Hi, honey! How's my baby girl?" Her mom smiled from ear to ear as soon as Janet swung open the door. "I'd give you a hug, but I got my hands full. Can you help me with these?" Janet's mom nodded toward the flower containers in her hands.

"Sure, Mom. What're you doing out and about this early?"

"Aw, I just thought it'd be the perfect day to plant some flowers and thought I'd surprise you, figured you'd still be in bed!"

Rather than inviting her mother in, Janet stepped outside onto the front porch. "Yeah, but why'd you bring roses?"

"Oh, I just saw these on sale at the store the other day, and I just thought about you and thought that these would look really pretty in the backyard. With fall coming along, we need to get them in the ground so they can get a good root system going before winter. Good to get them in the ground before it rains next week, too."

"Okay, Mom, well, if you want to. I didn't have anything planned for today. If you want to sit them down on the porch and come in, I was about to eat some breakfast. Would you like some pancakes?" she asked, stepping back inside the house and motioning toward the kitchen.

"Oh no, honey, I've already had some cereal at home," she answered as she followed Janet inside. "I'll just sit with you while you eat. Don't let me rush you."

The pair walked in the front door into the tiny foyer, the formal dining room on her left. Janet turned the corner to the right into the kitchen.

It was a cheery kitchen but rather plain. There was nothing special about the design, just a small galley layout with a breakfast nook nestled in the far corner where Janet's plate of pancakes beckoned.

"Oh, goodness, I thought you said pancakes! This is a full spread!" her mom said when she saw the table filled with pancakes, strawberries, whipped cream, syrup, peaches, and blueberries. "Oh, I'll definitely have some of that!"

"Help yourself," Janet said as she handed her mom a clean plate from the stainless steel dishwasher. As the two sat down and fixed their plates, Janet smothered her first pancake with syrup.

"Mmm, these strawberries are so good." Her mom moaned.

Janet smiled at her mom's indulgence. "I thought about you while I was cutting them up this morning because they're your favorite."

"They sure are." Sandra changed the subject. "Janet, you seem to be doing a little better. How's Marcus?"

"He's fine, same as usual. You know, we don't get to talk very much, and when we do, we really don't' have anything to talk about," she said. "My day, his day, blah. Anything else we want to know, we can see on Facebook. It just cuts out conversation. Why repeat something we both already know?" she questioned rhetorically.

"I've been thinking I should get me a Facebook," Sandra said, cleverly avoiding what was obviously a sore subject.

"You're not missing anything, Mom."

"Everybody talks about it so much. Even little Lucy wants to have a Facebook. My friend Rebecca at work even has one for her dog. I just think it's so silly."

"I do too!" They both concentrated on eating their pancakes for a few minutes.

"Honey, don't let it bother you so much when you guys don't have much to talk about." Her mom inserted now that Janet's moment of frustration seemed to have passed. "I'm sure you can think of something, like making plans for things you can do once he gets home."

"Yeah, but I don't like thinking about that stuff."

"Why not? It's going to be so exciting! He's going to get home, and you're going to get to make up for lost time."

"Yeah, but when he gets home, I'm still going to go to work every day, and he's going to go back to work after a few weeks. Life goes back to normal...whatever that is. There's not time to do a bunch of fun things."

"Okay." Her mother conceded. "But what about just being together? Won't it just make the basic things fun things?"

Janet shrugged.

"I know your dad and I have been together for a long time, but the little things are still good. We don't go on big vacations, we don't go on cruises, we don't have fancy dinners all the time, but we have dinner at the table together every night. Even if it's just fast food, we bring it home and eat it around the dinner table like it's a great meal, or we order in pizza or eat sandwiches because I don't have time to cook or pick up anything else." She paused and took a bite of a strawberry. "The point is that we're together. Won't that be nice?"

"I guess so, I haven't really thought of it that way." Janet admitted. "It's just so complicated. When I think of him sitting across the table from me, I just get lonely and miss him even more, or I get mad that he's gone. But we didn't even sit across the dinner table before he left, so why should I be mad that he isn't here to do it now? We just fixed our plates. I'd sit on the couch, him on the recliner, and we'd just watch TV while we ate. Why will it be any better when he gets home?"

"You should make a point to sit at the table. There's just something about gathering around the food and asking God to bless the meal and bless your family that is special, even when the meal itself is chicken nuggets. Family is still family, and time together is precious."

"We used to sit at the table together a long time ago. Sometimes I forget what it's like for him to even sit in the living room with me. You know, I'm going to have a hard time just going back to watching his TV shows! I've gotten so used to watching my kind of television shows, my girly movies and design shows and cooking network."

Janet's eyes got really wide as if she'd just seen a ghost. "I'm gonna have to start watching those swamp men and the ax people again!" she whined, dramatically hanging her head to convey her disappointment.

Sandra smiled and shook her head in understanding while laughing at her daughter's stunned reaction to the thought of watching Marcus's TV shows. "Your daddy likes watching those, too, sometimes." She chuckled. "But when Marcus gets home, you won't mind so much. You're going to be so glad that he's here, you aren't going to care what's on TV."

"Our conversations are pitiful, Mom. What do normal couples talk about? I've started to wonder if all we ever did was just watch TV...and talk about TV!" She giggled exasperatingly. "It just doesn't make sense. I can't remember what our conversations were like when he was home."

"It doesn't matter what they were like when he was home, honey. Things may not ever be like they were before he left. This year has done a lot to change both of you. You're a lot different woman than you were a year ago."

"Why do you say that?" Janet asked defensively, preparing herself for her mother's criticism.

"Well, I think you've seen what you can handle and how hard life is without him, and how lonely you can be without him. I think you're going to appreciate him being around a lot more. You've realized you can be independent, you can make it on your own...but that's not what you want."

"No, it's not"—she paused in thought—"I don't know what to expect, and I'm not happy with the way things are right now. I'm miserable. Things have been getting a little better in the last few weeks, but I'm sick and tired of being sad, lonely, or mad all the time. I'm trying to find stuff to do to keep my mind off things."

"Well, that's why I'm here. Let's clean up in here, and let's go outside and plant some roses!"

"All right, I have to change first. Do you mind putting the dishes and food away while I go change?"

"Sure."

Janet hurried to go put on her outside jeans—her "backyard britches" as she jokingly referred to them—her oldest pair of tennis shoes and a pink tank top.

"All right, let's get started," she yelled down the hallway as she stepped out of her bedroom.

Already headed out the backdoor, Sandra had on her gardening accessories, and Janet smiled. Her mom was so good with flowers and looked so cute in her sun hat and polka dot gloves carrying her pink bucket with her turquoise-handled set of gardening tools inside.

Janet stepped through the sliding glass door and pulled it closed behind her before opening the bench just outside the backdoor to retrieve her own gardening gear—an old pair of brown cloth gloves with a big hole in the seam between the thumb and left pointer finger, a hand shovel with a splintery handle, and the tip end of a hoe she used as a hand tool because the long handle had broken off. She threw a cap on her head and headed out.

Janet wanted to be like her mom, to have that nurturing maternal instinct that helped her create such beautiful flower beds. They were so much more than typical flower beds; rather, they were artistic flower arrangements in the dirt. A local magazine had even featured her yard in its "Best of the Neighborhood" segment a few years back.

Janet, on the other hand, couldn't arrange pretty flowers in a vase and keep them alive one day, much less envision the end result well enough to arrange mere seeds and prep them for months. She stuck to store-bought arrangements or single stems in glass cola bottles.

But her mom could do it, no question about it. Janet never really studied her mom's flowers when she was a little girl. They were simply a part of the home's decor. She didn't realize how much work went into them each day to keep the yard looking so beautiful. It didn't look like work when mom was deadheading the plants every other day or watering the ferns every afternoon.

The mother-daughter pair stepped off the porch into the backyard and picked up the delicate roses Sandra had sat out there.

"What kind of roses are these, Mom? They sure are pretty." Janet admired the muted yellow petals outlined in bright pink.

"They're peace roses," she answered. "I thought you would like them."

"They may very well be the prettiest roses I've ever seen. I love how the colors blend together like that," Janet said as she carried them over toward the empty flower bed lining the fence that separated her yard from her neighbor's.

"Yellow roses with a pink tip like this are supposed to symbolize falling in love. At least, that's what the lady at the nursery told me," she said. "Not sure why it's called the 'peace rose' if it means falling in love, and I started to pick a different kind, but then I thought about it. Falling in love is probably the happiest time of a woman's life, so I figured you could use a little of that happiness…and peace is always good."

Marcus had planted vegetables in that raised bed the year before, so they didn't have to do a lot of work to get it ready for the roses. Mother and daughter pulled weeds in silence for a while before the pair got their shovels and went to work digging small holes a couple feet apart.

Janet's mind drifted off thinking of how relationships were hard work sometimes too, much like digging in the dirt to plant flowers.

"Planting them is the easy part," Sandra broke the silence as she paused to remove her gloves and wipe the sweat from her forehead. "Yeah, the dirt may be hard when you first begin, but getting them in the ground and started—that's easy. It's nurturing them that's tough." She nodded to her daughter.

"You just have to water them," Janet said. "Keeping them alive shouldn't be that hard."

Sandra laughed. "I didn't say 'keeping them alive' is tough. I said 'nurturing them' is. Making the blooms flourish is what's difficult. To make a rose grow and be beautiful, you have to break off any dead blooms so new growth can appear. You have to water it regularly, fertilize the soil, spray for bugs, break off any insect-ridden leaves before the bugs spread to the rest of the plant. Having a beautiful, flourishing garden takes a lot of work," she said.

"Having a flourishing relationship takes a lot of work too," Sandra added maternally.

Janet thought about the point her mother was delicately trying to make. She and Marcus had been watering their relationship enough to keep it alive, but it had been a long time since their relationship had grown or flourished.

She could picture the roses in full bloom next spring all along the fence row and how beautiful her yard would be if she could maintain them, and she tried to picture her relationship next spring but couldn't. It was going to take a lot of work to tend to their relationship, make it grow, and make it something beautiful again.

As she and her mother finished packing the soil around each plant, Janet realized that it wasn't just her relationship with Marcus that she needed to tend to. She had a lot of weeds in her life that were preventing her from blooming where God had planted her, and Janet really wanted to flourish for him. Yet she had never made the effort to do more than simply stay alive, and her "just enough to get by" mindset needed to change.

Janet stretched out the green water hose from the faucet on the back of the house to water their newly planted roses while Sandra stretched out on the swing with a deep breath. She tossed her filthy gloves to the ground and let out a deep sigh.

"What's wrong, Mom?"

"Oh, honey, this weather. I'm glad we got these in the ground before the big rain next week. I don't like you being here by yourself when the storm hits."

"Are they saying we're going to get a lot of rain?" Janet asked. She caught glimpses of the news but didn't keep up with what was going on.

"I think so. The worst of the storm should miss us, but we should get several inches, at least," Sandra said.

"Well, I'll be fine," Janet said, trying to convince her mom. "Thank you for worrying about me, though."

"Well, you know I'm always here. I'll come whenever you need me. I'd rather be in pain myself than to see you hurting like this."

"I know, Mom," Janet said solemnly as she turned off the hose and joined her mom on the swing. "I'm okay. I really am, so you can stop worrying. Everything is fine."

Sandra patted her daughter on the knee, and Janet could see tears of concern in her eyes. "It's my job to worry about my babies. That's what mothers do. One day you'll understand."

Janet swallowed hard, wondering if she should tell her mother about the treatments, the failed attempts, wondering if she should share the agony and heartbreak she'd been handling alone for so long.

"Maybe so," she whispered, leaning her head on her mother's shoulder as they rocked back and forth on the swing.

As the steaming hot water streamed over her tanned body, she swore all her muscles were rebelling against her for putting them through so much strain in one day. Marcus and her mom had always been the gardeners whereas Janet would have rather looked at the pretty flowers or eaten the juicy tomatoes than plant and tend them any day.

Her body sure didn't like it either and was begging for a soak in a hot tub. *Too bad I don't have one of those*, she sighed as she turned off the showerhead and reached around the white curtain to the cotton towel draped over the wall hook. Her breath was still tight in her chest from being out in the heat; she probably should have taken a cold shower, but her muscles had demanded steam.

Breathing a deep sigh, Janet lazily adorned her lavender moisture-wicking nightgown, the cool fabric refreshing her sun-kissed skin, then sat on the edge of the white comforter to towel-dry her wet hair and rest for a few minutes before ransacking the pantry to find something to suffice as a late dinner, something besides a tomato sandwich.

Settling onto the couch with a bowl of cinnamon and pecan Special K and 2% milk, Janet reached for the satellite remote control, hoping—yet not expecting—to find something worthwhile to watch before she went to bed.

"Coming up on the nine o'clock news, we'll tell you all about—"

"No thanks," she muttered, quickly changing the channel. The newscasters never reported anything good, and Janet had enough negativity in her life to be worrying about the rest of the world's problems.

"How you doin'?" Joey nodded to her in his trademark way from the television screen in an old rerun of *Friends*.

"That's more like it." She heaved a sigh, wiggling to create a nest for herself in the oversized couch cushions while trying not to spill her cereal in the process, when the phone rang.

"Of course, as soon as I get comfortable," she muttered, knowing the only person who'd call this late would be her husband. While she did like to hear from him, she despised that their only contact was through a phone.

As she reached for the phone, Janet caught herself sighing and she half smiled. If he were here, Marcus would poke her in the ribs and say "Ugh" dramatically while rolling his eyes and theatrically shrugging his shoulders. She would try to keep a straight face, hiding the laugh that threatened to erupt, but could only succeed for a few seconds before letting a smile slip, getting the best of her stern resolve. Marcus always seemed to find ways to make her giggle in the midst of her most frustrating moments, a trait she desperately missed in his absence. Without him to soothe her aggravation and avert her mind from whatever issue assailing her, those same small daily frustrations overtook Janet's spirit.

"Hey!" she answered, making an effort to sound more upbeat than she felt.

"Did I wake you up?" Marcus asked. He could always heed the underlying tones of her voice, even when she tried to hide them. While he appreciated her effort trying to sound bubbly because he disliked calling when she was in a foul mood, she couldn't fool him; he knew she wasn't a perky person, especially near bedtime.

"No, I just sat down to eat supper and watch TV," she replied, turning down the volume on the television just as Rachel and Joey laughed at something Chandler said as he entered the coffee shop.

"It's a little late for supper, isn't it? What have you been doing?" Marcus inquired, drawing her attention away from the sitcom episode she'd seen multiple times.

She knew he was just making conversation, but her defenses involuntarily locked up as though he didn't trust her or thought she was just lazily sitting around doing nothing while he was away.

"I was planting flowers with Mom," she haughtily replied, "and I really thought the heat was going to get me today. It was awful out there."

Marcus's thunderous laughter blurted through the receiver. "You don't know what *hot* is!" he declared amid his chuckles. "You've got it made! Try wearing two layers of clothes in a 125-degree dust storm, then talk to me about *hot*," he said.

His comment might have been intended to make her realize how good her life was, but that wasn't how Janet understood it.

She hated when he said things like that, like his suffering was supposed to lessen hers or make her feel guilty. It may be 120 degrees in Iraq, but that didn't nullify the fact that 90 degrees in Mississippi was hot, too.

"Well, I know I can't handle hot weather, so I definitely wouldn't *volunteer* to spend a year in the desert like you did."

His jaw tightened. He wished her voice wouldn't pitch on that word *volunteer*, rubbing in the fact that he'd chosen to enlist and, thereby, chosen to leave her alone. He knew what that little jibe in her voice meant; he was no fool.

"What kind of flowers did you plant?" he asked through clenched teeth, trying to change the subject before another typical argument ensued.

"Peace roses."

"Oh," he said as though he knew what she was talking about.

"Honey, I'm sorry, but can we talk later? I'm really tired," Janet asked. Too often, she was half-asleep when he called. The time difference was hard to overcome some days, and she felt guilty for essentially blowing him off when their whole relationship revolved around these bits and pieces of phone conversations.

"Sure." He relented. "I understand. I have a lot I need to do this morning, but I wanted to call and wish you goodnight before you went to bed."

"Well, thank you. My body is so tired that I'll probably be asleep as soon as I hang up the phone."

"Good. I know you could use a good night's rest. I love you."

"I love you, too."

"Well, good night," Marcus said.

"And good morning to you. Have a good day," Janet replied and hung up the phone.

# Chapter 9

"Sing the wondrous love of Jesus, sing his beauty and his grace," Marcus sang along, relishing in the chance to sing an old hymn led by a Southern Baptist chaplain for once. He smiled as he tossed his head back and belted out in the way that he used to when he'd "sing and shout the victory" along with other soldiers of different denominations and levels of rank who were all joined together inside the tent one Sunday morning.

When the song had ended and they all sat in their folding chairs, Marcus picked up the leather case that held his Bible from the floor underneath his seat and unzipped the cover slowly to quiet the noise of the teeth releasing on the zipper.

"Today, we're going to look at the verses of Paul to the Philippians. Turn with me if you have your Bibles to chapter 4, verse 4. 'Rejoice in the Lord always, and again I say, Rejoice!' we read.

"Rejoice, it says." The chaplain paused, looking around and making eye contact with men and women across the tent.

"Always, it says!" His boisterous voice bounded as he enunciated his statement by pumping his fist in the air with each word. He looked toward the ceiling for a moment as his hand slowly sank to the small wooden podium where his dusty, worn Bible lay opened, and his demeanor changed, the excitement in his eyes turning grave. Solemnly, he looked straight in Marcus's direction when he said, "Keep. On. Rejoicing."

Marcus saw the chaplain's gaze turn to touch every soldier in the tent as he repeated those words again, but Marcus felt the man's words had been solely directed to him. Conviction besieged Marcus as he realized he hadn't been rejoicing in the Lord in a long time. Staring straight ahead and with eyes fixed securely on the wooden podium so as not to make eye contact with the chaplain again who would surely see the guilt in his expression, Marcus knew that one had to start rejoicing before one could keep on doing it.

As the chaplain continued to speak, Marcus dropped his head to read along in his Bible, which was laid across his lap. "Be careful for nothing; but in everything by prayer and supplication with thanksgiving let your requests be made know unto God." The chaplain stopped abruptly.

"Did you read that last part?" he asked. "Read it again: in *everything*, by prayer and petition, with *thanksgiving*. Thanksgiving, it says. Present your requests to God. When was the last time you prayed with genuine thanksgiving?"

The speaker hesitated, giving the soldiers time to ponder the rhetorical question. From where he sat, Marcus could see some soldiers drop their heads in apparent shame as they thought of how long it had been since they thanked their Creator; he saw some soldiers looking timidly at their neighbors to observe their reactions; some stared blankly ahead; a few nodded in agreement and muttered a muffled "amen."

"This verse tells us that in every circumstance, *every* circumstance, we should come to God with thanksgiving. What do you have to be thankful about today?"

As the chaplain continued his message about searching for and uncovering blessings in the midst of trials, Marcus contemplated everything he had to be thankful for.

His home needed a lot of upgrades, but it was in a safe neighborhood, and while the old heat pump sucked electricity like a leech, it kept the small brick house bearable in the hot summer and cozy in the winter.

He hadn't climbed the success ladder like he had once hoped he would in the financial world, but his coworkers at the bank were friendly and overall good folks. His relationship with his wife wasn't very solid, but she was a good woman, and he was lucky to have her regardless of the problems they had encountered over the past couple years.

Marcus figured that most of the other guys sitting around him were probably thinking the same thoughts as he. They all understood how being overseas in a war zone gave one mixed feelings about thankfulness. Some days were greater reminders than the others of just how blessed a man was simply to be living, breathing, and in one piece.

Other days, the ache in his gut would strikingly make him aware of how blessed he had been at home, and he longed for the menial problems of daily living with his wife. Drinking a cup of the flavored water the Post Exchange called coffee made him regret how angry he used to get when his work day got off to a rough start for spilling premium blend dark roast coffee on his three-piece suit while driving to work in his two-year-old SUV. Repeatedly carrying the tiny trash can from his room out to the community dumpster reminded him of the horrible smell at home every time he forgot to take the trash bag full of raw chicken packaging to the dumpster at the end of the driveway. Walking across the sand back to the barracks after a shower in the portable unit made him realize how blessed he had been to only have to walk a few steps to bed each night after taking a shower in his master bathroom. When he was at home, he had often muttered complaints as he crawled under the cotton sheets about how he could hardly turn around in the confining shower.

"And being thankful in the midst of difficult circumstances isn't always easy." The chaplain drew Marcus's attention back from his musings. "But you have to know that God is still God," he exclaimed, raising both of his arms in the air in praise. "Whether you are high on the top of that mountain where you have a clear view of the blessings of life all around you or whether you're down in the valleys of life and all you can see is the bumpy road ahead, God is still God. Let us pray as the scripture says in the next verse that 'the peace of God, which transcends all understanding, will guard your hearts and your minds in Christ Jesus. Amen.'"

As the soldiers all began to stand and move toward the exit at the back of the tent, Marcus stayed in his folding chair a few moments longer where he prayed in his heart that God would give him the peace mentioned in the scriptures, the peace he would never understand but would gladly welcome.

"Come on, Lucy! Wash your hands so we can eat," the fifty-two-year-old woman called, peeking her head around the doorway to the pigtailed five-year-old playing dress up with her dolls in the middle of the adjacent living room.

"I want Aunt Janet to help me." Lucy grinned as she skipped passed her grandmother into the kitchen, blonde hair and ribbons bouncing, and went over to Janet who was setting the table to tug on the leg of her pantsuit.

"Just a second, hold your horses," Janet teased as she placed the last utensil set next to its silver-rimmed plate before permitting the little girl to lead her hand in hand down the dimly-lit hallway lined with generations of old family photographs.

The two remaining women went back to putting their finishing touches on the Sunday dinner of shake-and-bake chicken, elbow macaroni and cheese, squash casserole, and purple hull peas.

"She sure does love having her Aunt Janet around," Sandra observed to her younger daughter while stirring the sugar into the tea after the other two were out of earshot.

"Yes, she does," the girl's mother replied as she took the casserole out of the stainless steel oven and turned the pan of chicken on the top wire rack before closing the door and turning the oven temperature down to 250 degrees. "She asks about Janet all the time, always wanting to know where Uncle Marcus is."

"Umm…that smells good," Sandra declared, breathing in the chicken's aroma that was quickly filling the small kitchen. "What do you tell her?" she asked her daughter Julia.

Taking a yellow ceramic serving bowl out of the maple cabinet over the microwave, Julia answered, "Well, in the beginning, we just said he was with the other soldiers." She paused to sit the bowl on the counter and began to carefully pour the peas into it, then continued. "But now that she's learning about maps in her kindergarten class, she wants a more specific answer, so I finally showed her one on the internet and let her point to Iraq," Julia remembered with a smile.

"I bet that helped," Sandra remarked.

"Oh, I thought so too"—the younger woman laughed, shaking her head as she recalled—"till we talked to him one night on the webcam. You should've seen her face when she turned to me wide-eyed and whispered, 'Mommy, how'd Uncle Marcus get in the 'puter?'"

The older woman let out a loud chuckle, shaking her head in amusement just as her daughter had done a moment before. "Out of the mouth of babes," she proclaimed with a laugh as their husbands came walking into the eat-in kitchen from the living room where the football game was still blasting away.

"What're you hens in here cluckin' about?" the older of the two men sniggered.

"Julia's just telling me how Lucy thought Marcus was stuck in the computer when she saw him on the online video," Sandra told her husband.

"Ya don't say!" He laughed, cocking his head to one side and forward a bit, wide-eyed looking just like his little granddaughter had on the day in question.

"It was pretty funny to hear her tell about it, too," Zachary explained, smiling as he began to tell them all about his daughter's amazement the morning after her video chat with her Uncle Marcus.

"Yeah"—Julia interrupted her husband—"she hardly touched her frosted flakes because she couldn't wait to get to school to tell Mrs. Black about her uncle in the 'puter with the other soldiers." Julia's hands swung around as she talked, gesturing wildly in her usual way as she told the story. As the little girl dragged a smiling Janet back into the dining room, Janet caught part of her sister's story and ducked her head to hide her grin as she pictured her sister being jerked around by strings attached to each arm, like a puppet being flopped around haphazardly.

"I kept telling her that Uncle Marcus isn't really in the computer, but you know how inquisitive she is. She just kept insisting he *was* because she could *see* him and *hear* him through the *scween*," Julia's bright blue eyes widened as she mimicked her daughter's persistence and mispronunciation of the word *screen*.

The family was still chuckling as they walked over to the table. The men pulled out their chairs to sit down at opposite ends of the table as the women carried the last of the dishes and sat them in the center on coordinating green and yellow pot holders.

"Come on, sweetheart, sit beside your Aunt Janet," Julia said while adjusting the pink booster seat on the straight-backed wooden chair.

"Yay! I wuv sittin' by Aunt Janet!" her voice squeaked before she ran over to the table to her chair.

"Don't run in the kitchen." Julia scolded.

"It's okay," Janet encouraged. "Come on, I'll help you get in your seat."

"I'll sit right across from you, so we can watch each other while we eat, okay?" Julia told her daughter as Janet picked the little girl up, helping her into the booster seat and scooting her chair closer to the table.

"See? I'm right here where you can see me," Julia said to her little girl who was paying her no attention.

"Do you want some peas?" Janet asked as she began fixing a plate for the child.

The usual Sunday chatter ensued as everyone began eating, passing the platters and bowls of food around the table as they had done for years.

The six-person table was full, but to Janet, it felt empty without Marcus in the seat beside her chatting with her dad and Zachary about yesterday's college football games and the much-anticipated BCS standings that would come out later that afternoon. The rather small rectangular table had been overcrowded after Lucy was born, and she'd sat in a highchair or booster seat at one corner of the table until Marcus had deployed, then her booster had been moved to his seat beside Janet, which rather conveniently left Aunt Janet with the task of getting the picky child to eat because reaching across the table to help her child with meals was too difficult for Julia.

While the men talked sports, Julia captured her mother's attention as usual with stories about Lucy while Janet accommodatingly fixed the little girl's plate, played airplane with a spoonful of peas trying to convince her to eat a few bites—

even though Lucy should have outgrown that game by this age—wiped her tiny mouth with the ivory linen napkin when more of the squash casserole ended up on her face rather than in her stomach, bent underneath the table to retrieve the napkin that had impishly been thrown to the floor in protest of the baked chicken Janet had torn into tiny bite-sized pieces; but at least Lucy ate her macaroni and cheese with no reluctance after her sidetracked mother paused just long enough from one of her stories to promise ice cream as a reward. As Janet scooped vanilla ice cream into a plastic red bowl a few minutes later, she wondered if Julia ever paid any real attention to her daughter at all.

"Well, I'm stuffed," Houston, Janet's dad, said with a satisfied groan, his fork making a loud *clink* as he sat it down on the plate. "That sure was good, ladies."

"Yes, it was." His son-in-law agreed. "I wonder what the score is," he commented as they both pushed their chairs back to retreat into the den where the football game was still playing.

When Janet and Marcus had first married, he would have stayed in the kitchen to help clear the table. The first time he had eaten dinner with her family, Janet remembered her mom nudging her side with an elbow then leaning over and whispering "he's a keeper" as she quietly pointed to Marcus at the sink doing dishes.

Somewhere along the years, the women had stopped bragging on his helpfulness in the kitchen, and then it stopped as he began joining the other men in front of the television as soon as the meal ended. Janet hadn't really even noticed the change.

"The preacher gave a really good sermon this morning, didn't he?" Sandra asked her daughters as the three of them still sat at the table, reluctant to get up and clear away the mess. "Whatever is true, noble, right, pure, lovely, admirable – think on these things. One of my favorite verses," she continued before taking a slow bite of the vanilla ice cream that topped a small slice of sour cream pound cake Julia had bought at the grocery store the day before.

"He did do a good job," Janet agreed, stirring her ice cream and watching it melt over the cake slice she had popped in the microwave to warm, careful not to make eye contact with her mom or mention the scripture to keep from being drawn in a long Bible lesson her mom often liked to give her daughters.

While Janet appreciated the concern, an hour of church was enough; she didn't need to hear another sermon on the same topic. Because of the negative feelings she harbored most days about the track her life seemed to be taking, Janet could only bear the life lessons—which she always viewed as criticisms—in small doses, whether they be from church, her mom, or anyone else. Small doses.

"You know, it's so true. When we keep our thoughts focused on Jesus 24/7 and all the good things he has done for us and all the wonderful things he has given to us, we're so filled with joy that there's no room for bad stuff to creep in," Sandra continued anyway, despite the lack of prompting from her daughters.

Seeing the way Janet avoided her gaze, Sandra pried, "Now, I know you don't always feel like you've got a lot to rejoice about since Marcus is gone, but you'd feel a lot better if you stop focusing on all the negative and start focusing on all the good."

"Don't lecture me, Mom. How many nights have you had to spend apart from Dad? How many days have you gone home to an empty house to be completely alone? You just don't understand what it's like," Janet defended her feelings.

Julia piped in, "Well, I don't see why you're so sad sometimes. Life's so wonderful!" She bolstered with a smile, gesturing with her spoon to emphasize her point.

"Yes," Janet turned to her sister, speaking slowly, struggling to keep her tone at an even level. "Your life is wonderful. Congratulations. You've got everything you want—husband at home every night, you don't have to work because he pays for everything, and you get to spend all day with Lucy. If I had your easy life, I'd be happy too," Janet replied, her defense mechanisms rising and unveiling the resentment she often felt toward her younger sister. "Leave me alone, please. You guys won't ever understand," she said quietly as she rose from the table leaving her cake and ice cream behind.

"Come on, Lucy, want to go play with Aunt Janet in the living room?" Janet asked her niece in a sweet voice, forcing a smile.

"Can we play with Ruby?" the little girl asked, referring to her red-headed baby doll.

"Sure, let's go play with Ruby," Janet said as she helped the little girl down from the seat. Turning to her mother and sister, she forced herself to apologize. "I'm sorry. I know you're just trying to help, but lecturing me just makes it worse." Janet let herself be led away to the other room to play with dolls, leaving the other two women to clean up the mess in the kitchen. She knew they'd spend the whole time whispering about her, how sad her life was and how she needed to get her act together. Janet had heard it all so many times over the last few months that she couldn't listen to it anymore.

Lucy came back from the toy box with two dolls, one for Janet and Ruby for herself. "Let's play makeover," she said as she handed Janet a comb then began brushing the red hair on her own baby doll. Marcus used to sit on the floor with Lucy and Janet playing with her stuffed animals or puzzles, but he never would have played makeover, Janet thought with a slight smile.

After styling the hair of both dolls, changing their fashion attire, and pretending to put blush and lipstick on them, Janet pushed herself up off the floor, stretching her arms in the air trying to loosen up her muscles from being in such a cramped position for so long.

"Aunt Janet's got to go home," she told her niece, who was rubbing her eyes sleepily. "And I think it's time for your nap, little girl." She grinned lovingly as she watched the little hand twirl one pigtail around in circles like she did when she was tired.

"I don't wanna nap," Lucy whimpered reluctantly and yawned.

"Well, come give me a hug and tell me bye," Janet requested, stooping down to the child's height and reaching out her arms. Lucy hurried over, squeezed her aunt tight, then went right back to playing with the dolls.

Janet walked into the kitchen where her mom and sister sat at the clean table sipping sweet tea and looking at magazines. As she picked up her purse from the bench by the door, she bid them both goodbye.

Her sister remained seated and returned the sentiment, but her mom got up from her chair and came over to Janet to give her a hug.

"Honey, you know I love you," the older woman whispered in her daughter's ear. "I've prayed for you, and I know that things are about to get better. Just hang in there." She patted Janet on the back a couple of times like she had done since Janet was a toddler.

"I know, Mom. I love you, too. I'll talk to you later this week," Janet said, feeling guilty for the way she hurt her mom's feelings earlier, but still wishing people would listen when she asked to be left alone. Good intentions didn't always produce happy endings.

# Chapter 10

*I prayed, and I know things are about to get better,* her mom had said. All the way home from Sunday lunch, Janet had contemplated her mother's words as she drove through town methodically stopping at red lights and braking at turns, hardly noticing the cars around her as though the car were driven by autopilot. Turning onto her street as she did every day, she noticed how busy her neighbors seemed to be—Larry cutting his grass, which never seemed to get tall enough to need cutting, Lisa hollering at her boys to stay away from the road with their game of Frisbee, someone's Chihuahua yelping, a couple she called "the joggers" because she didn't know them by name, and several ladies out watering their flowers like they did every afternoon around this time.

Suzanne, the gray-haired woman who lived next door to Janet, smiled and waved with her gardening glove, then went back to pruning the yellow and pink rose bushes that lined the front of her brick rancher as Janet turned into her own driveway. Janet waved back neighborly as she put the car in park.

As she closed the car door behind her and began walking toward the front door of her house, Janet didn't know whether or not she believed in answered prayers anymore, but her mom certainly did. Truthfully, Janet was afraid to pray for anything because she felt that every gift had a cost. "Be careful what you pray for," she'd always been told, and she, without doubt, took the sentiment to heart.

Janet's prayer life, or the lack thereof, was filled with fear. If she prayed for more free time, she might lose her job; if she prayed to tell God she couldn't handle any more trials right now, somebody she loved might get sick; and if she prayed Marcus would come home soon, he might come home in a wooden box. That last scenario terrified her most of all, so she just didn't pray. "Be careful what you ask for" made her wary of asking at all.

Janet knew from growing up in church that she should pray for God's will to be done no matter what, just as Jesus had prayed in the Garden of Gethsemane for the cup to be taken from him but then willfully accepted the cross since it was God's will. But she wasn't God. She knew the answer would be to "What Would Jesus Do?" but she couldn't do it. She wasn't strong enough to say *God, this is what I want, but it doesn't matter. Just do what you want in my life.* She really didn't see the point in praying for anything if God was ultimately going to do what he wanted anyway.

Yet she still prayed for God to keep Marcus safe. She didn't really think her words mattered to God, but she knew that even if they didn't help her words surely couldn't hurt.

She never prayed for herself anymore, though. Too many times during this deployment Janet had asked God for help, but he seemed to be ignoring her every request. Well, she knew the Bible said that God answered every prayer, big or small, so she assumed his answer to her pleas was always "no."

Janet pictured God sitting on his throne screening the calls on his cell phone, clicking "ignore" each time he saw her number on the caller ID. Or maybe Heaven had a front desk with an angel who routed all the calls and took messages for God, and Janet's messages were getting buried under a mountain of more important ones from people who actually mattered to God, people who were talented and had something special to offer.

He'd answer her calls eventually—*in his time* like the Bible said—but Janet feared his time would be too late to help her. She needed support and guidance right then, in that moment, not months from now after the deployment would be over.

Janet had always been impatient, a characteristic she had in common with her mom. Everyone said they both got it from her great grandma, a tiny woman who could do the work of three grown men without blinking an eye. Since Janet had grown up, she heard rather often how much she was like Janie, who would ask for help but then do exactly what needed to be done if the person she asked didn't stop right then and do what she had asked them to do. That ninety-pound woman could move a whole chifforobe down the hall to another bedroom by herself or chop down a tree that was shading her flower bed if no one jumped to do her bidding when she requested. But that was until she had gotten sick. Alzheimer's took away her strength and, as it seemed, doubled her stubbornness.

The stories she'd heard of her grandma's transformation after the disease took hold are what led Janet to her line of work at the nursing home. Janie had needed help. The family hadn't been able to provide what she needed at home, and they also couldn't afford a nursing home and wouldn't have sent her to one, anyway, even if they could because of the horrifying stigma of locking her away in a foreign room to die.

The sweet little lady had become violent, her mom had told Janet. More than once Sandra had been called to her parent's house in the middle of the night because Janie had tried to hurt herself or one of them. Janet was too young when her great-grandmother died to remember any of that, other than a picture she recalled of a frail woman with thin, unkempt hair whiter than the cotton fields in south Alabama where she'd grown up, sitting in a rocking chair on the back porch staring off into the woods for hours without a sound.

After she had died, Janet's parents had moved. Janet learned later that the only reason they'd stayed in Alabama her early years was to help with Janie. Her dad had wanted to move back to Mississippi where he'd gone to college.

Janet remembered her mom saying several times over the years that she would never pray for patience because she feared what she'd have to go through to get it. Janet agreed. Yet what could teach patience better than deployment, being separated for over a year from the person you swore to share your life with?

She knew there were worse things than deployment—like watching someone you love be stolen away by a disease—but she couldn't imagine a worse feeling than the loneliness and emptiness in her heart. She didn't know if she'd ever stop blaming God and blaming Marcus for making her feel this way.

*Things are about to get better*, she thought back again to her mother's words.

Her mom didn't understand, and how could she? She'd never been separated from her husband for more than a few days at a time, and even she admitted that before they'd had children she'd often run home to her own mother's house on those occasions because she couldn't stand to be at their house alone. She couldn't do it for a few days, but Janet had to do it for months.

*No one understands*, Janet thought as she set her bag down to insert the key into the deadbolt and give the back door a hip bump of encouragement. Sometimes she had to shove the door to open it—one of those things for which having a husband around the house would be useful. As she started to reach down for her purse and step across the threshold into the living room, a quick movement in the backyard caught her attention out of the corner of her eye.

For a brief second, Janet froze. Another downside to living alone was the fear of strangers, robbers, murderers…whatever her imagination conjured up at the time. Right now, all she could picture was a rabid dog biting a chunk out of her leg and leaving her there in the yard to die with no way of calling for help since Mrs. Suzanne would never hear her unless she had her hearing aid turned way up. The poor woman's hearing was worse than a bat's vision.

She saw the azalea bush do a little dance at the corner of the house and realized whatever or whoever had caused the movement was in the bush hiding from her. The figure in the bushes had obviously seen her, so she wasn't sure what to do. She could pretend nothing was wrong, hurry inside, and call the police, but she was scared to go inside the house and be trapped in case it was a maniac there to rob her, and she didn't want to be a scared little woman who called the police every time she heard a noise.

Taking the key back out of the lock, she slowly stepped backwards toward the carport, debating with every step whether she should just turn and run as fast as her short legs could take her to the car and drive away.

*Oh, Lord, what do I do?* she prayed in a panic. There. She finally prayed for herself, she thought sarcastically as she took another step backward, only to lose her footing and land square on her rear end.

He was on her before she could even realize she fell. "Help!" she squealed squeezing her eyes shut and balled up fists to protect her face. "Get off me!"

Just as quickly as he'd pounced, he let her go with a deep whine.

Janet opened her eyes to one of the prettiest basset hounds she'd ever seen sitting obediently at her feet, head cocked to one side, floppy chocolate-colored ears pitched forward as if to say "What did I do wrong?"

"Where'd you come from?" she asked roughly, already anticipating the bruises that would show up the next day from her fall.

The hound nudged and inched closer to her, sniffing her now grass-stained pants as she stood and brushed them off, feeling pretty foolish and glad no one was around to have seen her freak out episode. Her pants were probably ruined.

With hands on her hips, Janet stared down at her would-be assailant, unsure whether to run him off for scaring her half to death or to playfully tussle his floppy ears. "I guess you're probably hungry," she crooned, reaching out her open palm to gesture she wasn't going to hurt him. While his ribcage wasn't showing under the dirty brown and white coat, she could tell he hadn't eaten a decent meal in some time, probably had been digging through her trash can when she'd gotten home judging from the looks of his nose and front paws.

"I don't have any dog food, boy," she apologized as she mentally surveyed everything in her fridge and pantry trying to think of something to feed the poor fellow. Bread? *No, he needs something better than that.* Canned tuna? *Do dogs eat fish or is that just cats?* Pizza? *Heck no, I'm not cooking for the dog.*

"Stay right here," she barked pointing her finger at the ground, then hurried inside through the open front door to the kitchen. Two minutes later, she came out with a can of cold beef stew on a paper plate.

"Here you go." She offered as she set the plate down on the dry grass, surprised that the hound hadn't moved an inch while she'd gone inside. The hungry fellow had actually done as she'd commanded and sat right where she told him to stay.

He attacked the plate as soon as it left her fingers, gobbling up every chunk of beef, potatoes, and carrots in barely a minute, then licked every tiny remnant of taste from the flower-rimmed plate before looking up at her expectantly as though to say, "Please, sir, I want some more."

From the beckoning pull of those dark chocolate eyes, Janet knew she was going to need a lot more beef stew.

"What am I going to do with you, huh?" she asked, kneeling down to the pup's level and reaching out her hand. "I don't know anything about puppy dogs," she admitted, crinkling her nose at him like *I Dream of Genie*, except that Janet couldn't wiggle hers back and forth.

Janet had never owned a dog. Unlike most children, she'd never asked her parents for one. A lot of her friends had pets growing up, but Janet had thought that taking care of one would be a lot of trouble. Considering the trash bag contents scattered around her knocked-over garbage can at the corner of the house, Janet assumed her childhood assessment had been right.

She couldn't call the pound since it was a Sunday, and the happy gleam in his eyes, his tongue hanging out on one side of his mouth hassling with joy and drooping ears bouncing like Lucy's pigtails with every energetic step he took won Janet over. She couldn't turn him over to the pound to leave his fate up to the system. She'd have to find him a good home.

*First thing tomorrow morning*, she thought.

"So what are we going to do about you tonight?" she asked him, putting her hands on her hips as she stood up from her kneeling position in front of him. His tail wagged back and forth swishing like a broom over the grass. "Will you stay here outside by yourself?" she asked as though she expected an answer. "You're too dirty to come inside."

The hound cocked his head and looked toward the door as though saying, "But please. I'll be good, cross my heart."

Janet pictured the puppy dog crossing his heart with his paw, and she couldn't help herself but be won over by his cuteness.

"I guess I could give you a bath," she responded rather reluctantly, not having a clue how to bathe a dog or how he would react to being doused in water. "Will you let me give you a bath?" she questioned, eyebrows raised in doubt.

The dirty hound sprung up, tail wagging so fiercely Janet feared he was going to hurt himself. She laughed at his excitement, thinking he had no clue what he was getting into. "All right, then. We'll try." She ceded. "Let's see what we can do about all that dirt."

She motioned toward the door. "Wanna go inside, boy? Huh? Wanna get a bath?" she asked in animated baby talk as she leaned over with hands on her knees and shook her head cooingly with eyes wide open, like the way she had talked to eight-month-old Lucy when she coaxed the tot to walk for the first time.

Responding cooperatively just as she'd hoped, the filthy pup followed Janet through the backdoor. He paused once inside to sniff around the living room, and Janet watched him walk over to each piece of furniture like a detective surveying every inch of a crime scene. Obviously finding whatever clues he required, the hound shook his floppy ears and walked over to Janet, allowing her to lead him down the hallway to the bathroom where the tub awaited.

"Gotta give me a minute to run the water and find you a towel, okay?" she sweet-talked, holding her hand out, palm facing him like the "Don't walk" hand that flashes at crosswalks. He obediently sat on the linoleum floor in front of the vanity cabinet and intently observed Janet fumbling with the faucet on the porcelain tub with one hand while still holding up the other for him to stay to make sure he didn't get into any trouble while she was distracted.

Warm water started to fill the tub, and she backed towards Marcus's cabinet where she kept spare towels while still holding up her hand toward the dog. She didn't want to mess up one of her fluffy ivory ones on a dog. His gaze watched her every movement, and Janet could tell he was on high alert wondering what was going on.

"All right, boy. Here goes nothing." She shook her head as she crouched down on the floor, knees resting on the folded-up towel by the bathtub. The hound walked right over to her and put his right paw on her leg. "Whew, you are a sack of taters!" she exclaimed as she scooped up the thirty-pound dog and sat him over into the water.

Still as a statue, he stood while she lathered her jasmine-scented frizz control shampoo into his coat, rubbing gently and quietly cooing soft reassurances and at the same time anticipating being drenched in doggy water if she didn't keep him calm.

But he just stood there, belly deep in the water, letting her splash all around him as she attempted to wash the dirt from every inch of his hair without making a huge mess. The tips of his floppy ears touched the water occasionally, and Janet could tell by the way he tossed his head that he didn't like his ears in the water.

"I'm sorry, boy. I'll try not to let them get too wet." She apologized while trying to hold his drooping ears up on top of his head while she scrubbed under his throat and around his chin. His ears were so long, and Janet pictured herself tying them together in a Minnie Mouse-style bow on top of his head.

Finally satisfied that he was as clean as she could get him, Janet let the water drain out; making a mental note to scrub the tub before taking her shower later as she noticed the filth left behind on the porcelain.

"Ah!" she squealed as he started to shake the water off, slinging water everywhere before she could grab the towel from under her knees and throw it over his back. "You got me!" She laughed as she wiped drops of water off from her face and shirt.

After wrestling with the towel to dry him off while the pup continued to shimmy the water off from its body, Janet went to her closet to change her clothes and ponder what to do with him for the night.

"Well, boy, do you have a name?" she asked, standing with her hands on her hips.

"No, I guess not. Well, what am I going to call you for now, huh? I can't just call you *boy*," she wondered out loud as she watched him lie down in the doorway of the closet to watch her get dressed, his droopy mouth smiling up at her and tongue hanging to the floor.

"You sure do look happy sitting there," she said. "All right, Mr. Happy it is. Come on, Mr. Happy. Let's go watch some TV."

As though he understood, he got up from the carpet and followed Janet back into the living room he'd earlier inspected so thoroughly. He walked straight over to Marcus's recliner and lay on the floor beside it, looking for Janet to join him.

"Okay, I'll sit there," she said, walking over to join him. His head followed her as she sat down in the chair and kicked up the footrest, and then he rested his snout on his crossed paws letting out a deep, satisfied moan as he closed his eyes.

Watching his back rise and fall steadily as he drifted off to sleep, Janet decided to join him in a nap. Curling up on her side and closing her eyes, a slight smile formed on her lips thinking how much Marcus would scold her for having a dog in the house.

# Chapter 11

"Eight. Nine. Ten," Marcus puffed, counting the last few reps before sitting the barbell back in its place above the weight bench. Sweat dripped into his face when he sat up to reach for his workout towel at the foot of the bench he was sitting on. Straddling the bench, he propped his elbows on his knees and wiped the sweat from his face and shoulders.

"Come on, man! You look like you done give out already," his buddy, Joshua, taunted him as they walked over to the rack of dumbbells against the wall and picked up a set of twenty-fives.

"I 'bout have," Marcus breathlessly replied, still resting between sets. "Man, I think I'm getting old. Better watch out—it's gonna happen to you someday too. This age mess sneaks up on you when you aren't looking," he warned with a smile and a nod to the other soldier, who was only a year or so behind Marcus.

"Dude, I got old the day my youngest turned two. Something about those terrible twos turns a man's hair gray, I'm telling ya." Joshua joked, running a hand over his shaved head. "Having another one starting kindergarten the same time sure didn't help any either. When you're chasing around a toddler while trying to help a kindergartener sound out a sentence, then come talk to me about feeling old."

The conversation stalled as both men became lost in their own thoughts—one missing his children, the other trying to overlook the fact that he had no children to miss.

Marcus used his towel to hide the expression on his face. The subject of kids was always a sore one for him. He'd always wanted children, but he couldn't imagine being one of these guys thousands of miles away from their babies. A man was supposed to be the leader of his home, and he didn't understand how he could do that without being present.

As much as Marcus would hate leaving his kids at home for months on end—worrying about how they were getting by without him, guilty for not being there to meet them at the school bus, fearing they would forget his voice or how much he loved them. Those proud, happy expressions on the faces of other soldiers when they opened a care package and pulled out a picture drawn with scribbled crayon made Marcus envious.

While he knew their burdens of being away from their children could be devastatingly trying, Marcus wanted his heart to one day beam with pride and delight like those of the other dads. He wanted it so much that sometimes he could hardly stand it.

He lay back on the bench and reached for the barbell to start another set, determined to focus his attention elsewhere by counting each thrust out loud.

One, *why'd he have to bring that up?*

Two, *Lord, I can't change it now.*

Three, *this is what I chose.*

Four, *would I've done it differently?*

Five, *would I've had kids instead?*

Six, *probably not.*

Seven, *I wonder if she'd do it differently.*

Eight, *she probably doesn't even think about it.*
Nine, *everybody else does it, I could've, too.*
Ten, *oh, well.*
*It's too late now,* Marcus thought discouragingly as he shook his head and determined to focus on his workout.

The sun was shining really brightly that Monday morning. She flipped down the visor, unclipped her sunglasses, and slipped them on trying not to mess up her hair as she drove to work. She thought back to the books she'd read, the descriptions of the sun, and remembered how corny she thought they sounded as she'd read them. But today the sun seemed to fit those vivid descriptions—the gigantic ball of fire igniting her soul.

Yet it didn't ignite her soul the way the dramatic novels described. The sun just made her sad, just made her wish Marcus was home, so they could go to the beach together. Her friends on a day like today would pack up the kids and head down to the beach to enjoy the warm weather while it lingered, even though the water had started to cool off this time of year.

Of course, her friends might invite Janet, and Janet could tag along, listen to this mom either complain about her children or brag about them. Sometimes even in the same sentence she could do both while secretly Janet wished it was her tugging along the two children and all their swimming gear, picturing herself with a little boy and girl in tow, putting on their sunscreen while they wiggled and tried to get away and carrying the cooler full of juice boxes. But instead, she'd just sit and watch her friends' kids play in the water and build sandcastles.

Janet remembered the summer of their second anniversary. Marcus surprised her with a spontaneous trip to the beach but forgot to make reservations, so when they got to the coast, they drove from hotel to hotel looking for a place to stay where they could afford a room and still afford to eat for the weekend while they were away. Frustrated, he had finally whipped in the parking lot of a super nice hotel with a vacancy sign out front, parked under the awning at the front entrance, went in, paid for the room and hid the receipt so she wouldn't know how much it cost.

She'd been so mad about that. If he'd just gone online, he could've found a nice room at an affordable price, but instead they'd wasted an hour and a half looking for a place to stay and wasted probably a hundred dollars more than necessary on a room. But, of course, she didn't know how much they wasted because he hid the receipt.

She wasted a lot of time being mad in that trip. Looking at the bright morning sun and remembering how pretty the weather had been that weekend eight years earlier, Janet thought about how she was wasting a lot of time being mad now too. She couldn't help it, though. Everything upset her. The tiniest mishaps frustrated the heck out of her. Janet didn't want to be miserable despite Marcus's assertions that she enjoyed being unhappy.

*Who would actually enjoy being unhappy?* she wondered. He said she enjoyed making him feel bad. Perhaps, that was partially true. She didn't want to *make* him feel guilty, but she did think he should feel that way sometimes for leaving her. She wasn't really sure what she wanted other than the fact that she just wanted him to be home.

But after months of arguing and being angry, she really wasn't sure she even wanted him to be home anymore. She didn't know how things would work out, and the uncertainty of their future scared her. She'd spend many sleepless nights pondering what would happen if he came home and they couldn't work out their differences. People talked like she should be able to let the negative times go easily, but they didn't understand how deeply she had been hurt by his deployment, how abandoned she'd felt when she needed him most after the fertility treatments were over.

Maybe that feeling of abandonment was why she wanted to keep Mr. Happy around. As she was brushing her hair that morning, he sat quietly on the bathroom rug behind her, and the look in his eyes in the reflection of her make-up mirror tugged at her heart as though he knew she were about to leave him there alone.

She almost called in sick to work because she felt sick leaving him, worried he may not be there when she returned, that he may go off looking for someone else to take care of him when she didn't return in just a couple of hours. Someone had neglected him too, and she didn't want to make him feel unloved or unwanted like she had felt the last couple of years. But she had to go to work, which meant he had to stay in the backyard unattended, and she just had to hope he was there when she returned that evening.

As Janet made her rounds, worried thoughts of Mr. Happy at home alone flooded her mind all morning. She tried to focus on her work and her patients, but blocking out his floppy ears and chocolate eyes was harder than she'd imagined.

"Hey there, young lady." An aged man in the wheelchair grinned as Janet, wheeling around her cart of medicine and supplies, approached the foursome playing cards on the back terrace in the middle of the morning. "Yer just in time fer the fun!"

"Oh, no, Frank. What are you up to now?" Janet cautioned with a wide grin on her pale face as she slowly approached the table circled by the group of men shuffling cards. Frank, Johnny, Bill, and Tom could be found outside playing card games nearly every morning since Janet had been working at the Springing Hills Rehabilitation Center.

These four men were often the highlight of her day since Marcus had deployed. Although she'd never admit it to anyone, the attention she got from these four seventy-something-year-olds was the only male attention she got these days—except, of course, for the encounter with the handsome stranger at the restaurant, the thought of which flustered her a bit. To be called pretty every now and then felt good no matter who said it.

"We're just getting a poker game goin'. Wanna join?" Frank cheerfully appealed, knowing of course that she wouldn't. His perfect dentures almost sparkled in the early morning sunlight as he beamed up at her like a five-year-old hiding a frog in his pocket and ready to throw it on the next unsuspecting pretty little girl he saw on the playground. Even in his old age, he considered himself a ladies' man. Janet had to admit that he did seem to make the little gray-haired ladies swoon, but Janet guessed their faint reaction was probably the result of his heavy "old spice" more than anything else.

"Mr. Frank, you know I don't have any money. I'm a nurse, for goodness sake, not a millionaire like you," she joked lightheartedly.

"If you play, we don't have to play for *money*," the retired farmer sitting next to Frank quipped with a wink. "We can play strip poker!" he exclaimed, bringing a roar of masculine laughter from the other three sitting at the round wrought iron table on the courtyard patio.

"Mr. Johnny, you dirty old man, behave yourself and act like you've got some raisings." She scolded and gave the old man's shoulder a good-natured swat.

"We may be old, honey, but we ain't dead," Bill said amid his bellowing laughter, slapping his knee in the cliché way men did when they said something they thought was funny. Janet noticed a slight wince as he slapped his knee and thought of his recent incident. She was glad to see him up and about after the fall he'd had a couple weeks earlier. He'd earned a ride on the ambulance for fear he had broken a hip, but luckily the damage was no worse than a deep bruise. She doubted he would be getting up to walk around his dark room in the middle of the night without his walker again anytime soon, though.

"Got that right! My eyes ain't as good as they used ter be, but lookin' at purdy girls is what God made glasses fer!" Frank chimed in, still grinning from ear to ear as he pointedly tilted his glasses in her direction, then nudged Tom who was sitting to his right.

"Ha-ha, good one," Janet dryly taunted as she turned to check on the patients at another table. Frank, Johnny, and Bill were in high spirits as usual, but she worried about Tom. He was the quiet one of the bunch, just sitting back, laughing when the others told jokes but without much comment of his own since his wife passed away a few months back. Janet pondered if he'd ever been much of a talker before her death either but couldn't recall.

Other than the daily poker game, Tom had spent most of his time by his wife's bedside during her last several weeks. She'd suffered like many of Janet's patients from Alzheimer's, but she'd always known who Tom was. Her short-term memory was nonexistent, causing her to forget basic things such as whether or not she'd already eaten lunch that day or which of her children or neighbors had visited her the day before.

Janet had conversed with Tom one-on-one quite often during those last weeks, mostly listening as he told her all about their lives before Alzheimer's. During the early days of the disease, he explained how his wife would mark the calendar on their side-by-side refrigerator to keep track of the days, but eventually she began to mark it twice in one day or not at all because she couldn't remember whether or not she'd already crossed out that day.

Eventually, she woke up one morning and put on one of her best dresses to go to church, only to have her frustration build as Tom attempted explanation that it was actually Friday, not Sunday. She didn't understand why her calendar said it was Sunday and insisted it was his mistake. She did it like she was a child throwing a temper tantrum over a piece of candy taken away by her father, which was somewhat understandable since going to church was the highlight of her week.

Tom had finally been forced to make the difficult decision of sending the love of his life to the nursing home after she caught their stove on fire from leaving a pot of tea boiling one night before bed. Fortunately, their children had insisted Tom have a fire extinguisher ready in the kitchen because they anticipated her forgetfulness would eventually cause a disaster like that. Unable to live apart from his childhood sweetheart, Tom sold his brick home of fifty-three years and joined her at Springing Hills where they'd lived nearly two years before she went home to the Lord.

During her last days, she recognized no one, and Janet recalled sadly the agony on Tom's face as he prayed for God to just take her and end her struggles. The day after her funeral, Tom's face seemed ten years younger whereas Janet had expected him to look tormented. She understood, however. His wife had been gone long before she died, and the look on his face could have easily been read as relief—relief that she was at home with her Father and no longer burdened by her bodily disease as well as relief that he no longer had to watch her suffer.

Sometimes, in her lowest moments when her loneliness crushingly weighed down her spirit, Janet had wished for similar relief. She simply did not know how a person could bear getting up each morning and going through this tired old routine just to go home to an empty house, crawl into an empty bed, and lie awake another night wishing for a different life.

But today, she wasn't going home to an empty house if Mr. Happy was still there waiting for her in the backyard where she'd left him. That thought lifted her spirits a bit, making her eager to get home rather than dismayed.

Her body physically ached from her unhappiness and loneliness at times. Her weight had ticktocked from one extreme to the other, like the metronome she used to keep time as she practiced piano years ago. One day, she'd binge on everything in the pantry, fridge, and freezer; the next, she'd forget to even eat. The Salvation Army downtown had become her go-to store because she couldn't afford to keep buying brand new clothes that would fit one week and not the next.

*At least, these unflattering scrubs fit no matter how much weight I gain,* she thought as she tugged the hem of her cotton-poly blend top, thankful for the wonderful invention of elastic and drawstring waistbands.

A movement in one of the windows caught Janet's attention. She squinted in the sunlight to see Lucille standing by her window, eyes intent on the roses being watered by one of the grounds keepers.

In the Mississippi heat, Janet knew it was best to water plants in the morning before the day starts, so she was surprised the gardener hadn't completed that task earlier. She hadn't watered her own roses either and made a mental note to do that before work the next day. If one waited until the afternoon or evening, the plants would have already suffered and wilted in the heat of the day.

The same is true of one's relationship with God, Janet's next door neighbor had once told her when Janet commented on the woman's daybreak routine of watering her roses. She'd turned it into a life lesson Janet had never forgotten, a lesson explaining how people need to start every day with a dose of the living water just as the plants need physical water to start each day with and thrive.

"A woman needs to saturate herself with his glory and his presence to fill her need for him throughout the day. Otherwise, you'll be like my thirsting roses, leaves drooping under the midday sun, spirits wilting under the pressure and challenges of the day," Mrs. Suzanne had lightly said as she plucked yellow leaves from her bushes while Janet had visited to return a cake stand she had borrowed for a party at church.

After Mrs. Suzanne had explained it so colorfully that day in her front yard, Janet had noticed that her own spirit did, in fact, need nourishment throughout the day just as her body needed food and drink. She'd taken the older woman's advice and began starting her day with devotionals, and she acutely began to notice a difference in her attitude on days when she missed waking up with God for whatever reason, regardless whether she overslept or just didn't take time to sit down with her Bible because she was stressed about tasks that she needed to complete that day.

When one goes too long without a meal, the physical body aches, the stomach pangs to tell the brain that the body needs food. With her relationship with God, Janet's spirit sent similar signals to her brain through the day reminding her when she'd missed her spiritual breakfast. One's spirit needs to hear the word of God, needs the Bread of Life, just to make it through the day.

That's how she had gotten through months of fertility treatments; although Janet had missed a lot of those spiritual meals and midday snacks over the last year or so; and her relationship with God had become depleted, functioning off of mere pockets of stored-up teachings of faith rather than daily; being replenished as it needed.

"Hey, doll, where'd you go?" Bill said, waving a hand of cards to draw Janet's attention back to the table of men.

"Sorry, I got distracted. Guess I'm a little out of it this morning," she replied, turning her cart back toward the table. "Well, I better get back to work," she added, making an overly dramatic frown and shrugging her shoulders with her bottom lip slightly poked out, which made all the old men laugh just as she'd hoped it would.

"Ah, well, don't work too hard, missy," Johnny said, followed by a chuckle from Frank as he said, "Come on back when you start missin' me." Tom just smiled and tipped his head as she passed.

Janet heard Bill begin telling a loutish joke while he dealt the next hand of cards behind her as she walked through the doors to visit her other patients. She caught only bits and pieces of it, something about a newlywed man laying down the law and his new wife saying she'd have dinner ready at seven o'clock every night, or something like that. Janet didn't hear enough to understand why the old men all burst into laughter, but she smiled as she turned the corner. Just hearing their loud chuckles made her feel good.

*Chapter 12*

After her chat with the old men on the terrace, Janet had finished her morning rounds meeting the various needs of her patients with no mishaps, and her day seemed to be going pretty well. Lunchtime, however, was rather eventful, if one considered spilled trays and spaghetti stains eventful. Janet assisted patients with their meals each day, yet she made a mess trying to feed herself. Even the patients with moderate tremors made less of a mess than she did today.

Janet was looking forward to banana pudding from the cafeteria, one of her favorite dishes they served and which always reminded her of the story her mom told about how Janie had forgotten to put bananas in the pudding one day after her Alzheimer's had kicked in. The old woman had served the family her signature dish minus its main ingredient and never even realized her oversight. That's when the family had known the disease had worsened, the "beginning of the end" as Sandra described it.

Carrying the green tray of spaghetti, salad, garlic bread, and banana pudding into the nurses' lounge to enjoy her thirty-minute lunch break peacefully, Janet was walking toward the rickety table in the far corner of the room when the door to the nurse's restroom flung open in front of her. She sidestepped around the door and thought she was in the clear until her toe caught the corner of the area rug and threw her off balance.

As if in slow motion, Janet flailed around trying to catch herself and not spill the food on the tray in the process.

An obscenity spouted from her mouth as the tray hit the floor, scattering spaghetti noodles across the floor and pudding down the right side of her shirt and pants leg.

"Oh gosh, I'm sorry," the nurse who had come out of the bathroom so abruptly said as she paused from texting to look at Janet and the mess on the floor. "I wish I could stay and help, but my break is over," she feigned a disappointed look, then went back to texting as she walked through the door to the lounge and into the hallway, leaving Janet alone with the spaghetti disaster.

Janet huffed as she grabbed a roll of paper towels from the cabinet under the bathroom sink, shut the cabinet door not so gently, then trudged back toward the strewn noodles. "Let's see if you're really a quicker picker upper," she challenged the roll of paper towels in her hands.

Janet's absentmindedness often resulted in bumping into things and making messes; and thanks to her tendency to bruise easily; some days she went home black and blue head to toe from uncoordinated encounters with medicine carts, wheelchairs, food tables, or sometimes even people. But this time wasn't her fault, yet she was still the one with a mess to clean.

"Story of my life," she muttered under her breath, frustrated that she couldn't have a single good day without something negative happening to put a damper on her spirits. Today, she actually had something to look forward to when she got home, so she didn't want to let some spaghetti stains ruin what had begun as a good day.

After swabbing up every drop of sauce and her beloved pudding, Janet had then spent the second half of her lunch break alternately rubbing her scrubs with soap and then rinsing with water as she tried to get the stains out of her uniform before the tomato-based sauce had time to set in. Needless to say, she hadn't had time to retrieve a second tray of food from the cafeteria before the second part of her shift began, so her stomach had been growling annoyingly all afternoon.

The afternoon dragged on longer than most, which was typical of a Monday. The weekend just passed, but she could still smell her Saturday morning hot chocolate slowly coming to a boil on the glass-top stove while she waited barefoot in her ragged cotton pajamas. In just a couple more hours at work, she'd be taking a trip to the grocery store to pick up some real dog food for Mr. Happy then be home in time for *Friends* reruns and a quick sandwich—unless something else tweaked her appetite at the store, which was very likely considering the noises her belly kept making in protest of missing lunch.

Her stomach was still growling later that day as she stood in the checkout line at the grocery store.

*Come on!* Janet screamed silently while giving the impatient evil eye to the young cashier with the blue-streaked hair, who put more effort into smacking her bright pink bubble gum than swiping the grocery items across the barcode scanner. The tapping of Janet's toe didn't have an effect on the college student behind the register, but every tap heightened Janet's blood pressure by a bit.

"Oh, dear, what happened to your shirt?" a sweet voice from behind Janet interrupted her toe tapping.

Janet turned to face the white-haired woman who was smiling warmly, yet with a wrinkled brow, as she scrutinized the spaghetti stains on Janet's uniform.

"I'm just a klutz," Janet muttered as she hastily pushed a gallon of stain remover, lavender-scented laundry booster, and dog food closer to the scanner trying to get the clerk to speed up.

"That looks like a bad stain. Make sure you soak your shirt in warm water, not hot," the older woman recommended. "Heat sets stains, you know," she said, nodding her head in a matter-of-fact way and scrunching her brows to emphasize the importance of her advice.

"If bleach doesn't get it out, I'll just throw it away and buy another." Janet resignedly shrugged.

"Oh, no, dear, you can't just throw it away!" the woman contended with shock in her voice. "I remember when people only bought new clothes for Christmas and couldn't imagine throwing away a perfectly good piece of clothing just because of a little stain. You can't just toss aside something that's messed up when a little effort could make it just like new again." She counseled with a look of disapproval in her soft blue eyes.

"I'm not going to throw it out without at least trying." Janet defended herself, wishing the blue-haired twerp behind the counter would just ring up her purchase, so she could drive home to see if Mr. Happy had waited for her. She was so worried that he would be gone—so worried that her hopes had gotten up for nothing—and really expected to be disappointed when she got home, but she hung on to a tiny shred of hope that he would be there in the backyard where she'd left him that morning.

Were Janet to be honest with herself, she would rather just throw the shirt away than fail to get the stain out. Replacing what is broken can often be easier than fixing it. The thought of starting over a whole new life somewhere far away and of giving up on her broken marriage after Marcus had betrayed her trust and thrown away the future they'd always planned to have together danced in her conscious mind for months after he was redeployed, but Janet didn't know if she could ever do it. When she thought about it seriously, she didn't see much point in starting over and building a brand new life. For her, a new life would just bring new problems, and the known demons are easier to deal with than the unknown.

"Come back to see us," the cashier finally said, handing Janet her receipt and change. She started grabbing the bags in her left hand as she stuffed the change in the right pocket of her scrubs and hurried away so quickly she almost missed the old lady's sincere smile and "good luck" as she rushed out the door to the parking lot.

The grocery store had been crazy that afternoon, which always seemed to be the case when all Janet wanted was to get in, find what she needed, and get out. Today, she could hardly even make it down the aisles because there were so many people.

*More typical of a Friday afternoon than a Monday*, she thought. As she hastened across the parking lot looking for her car, Janet heard someone call her name from the next aisle over.

"Janet! Hey! How are you?" Janet was greeted by the smiling face of a fellow military wife whose husband was in the same battalion as Marcus. The blonde-haired woman looked like she'd just stepped out of a salon with her waves perfectly bouncing around her face as she casually placed her sunglasses on top of her head. Two small children followed her obediently, one on each side holding her hand as the trio walked in Janet's direction.

"Hi, Kirstin," Janet responded, trying to fake a smile while kicking herself for not walking to her car faster. The exasperatingly positive blonde woman was great to have around working at bake sales, decorating for parties, or organizing a girls' night out, but Janet didn't have an hour to lose catching up in the parking lot, and she knew that Kirstin could ramble long enough to have her own talk show without the need for guest appearances.

"Oh, gosh, someone had a little accident," Kirstin teased, pointing at Janet's messy scrubs with her manicured finger. "That's going to make a bad stain," she said, with eyes wide and brows raised.

"Yes, I know. It's been one of those days."

"I'm sorry, honey," she frowned. "I understand. Between chasing these two around and keeping up the house, I sometimes just want to hide myself in the closet, but I'd probably just end up organizing my shoes!" Kirstin laughed as the blonde twin girls danced around her tanned legs.

"Probably so," Janet sighed with a half smile as she shifted the weight of the grocery bags on her arm impatiently, wondering how long she'd have to stand there in the parking lot faking a smile before she could politely escape to her car.

"What have you been up to lately?" Kirstin asked before quickly bending down to her two giggling daughters and harshly whispering, "Stop that! Mommy's talking to a friend." She then smiled back up at Janet to silently mouth "I'm sorry" and shake her head.

Janet watched the two little girls longingly. She and Marcus had put off having children for years because of his military involvement. Janet didn't want to face the struggles of being a single mom while her husband was thousands of miles away for months on end.

She admired those women who seemed to do it so effortlessly—juggling work and soccer practice, packing lunches and dance bags, locking the bathroom door just to get a few seconds of privacy, all without the help of a husband around—but until recently Janet had never wanted to be one of them. While those moms were struggling to fill dual roles, at least their homes weren't empty like hers. She'd gladly trade the silence of her home for the chaos of theirs any day.

"We should get together sometime for a girls' night, go to dinner or a movie. I don't know about you, but sitting at home on Friday night is getting *blah*." She giggled as she stuck out her tongue and rolled her eyes with that last word in a gesture, looking much like the blonde-haired children at her feet. "I can only watch so many Disney movies before I go *crazy*," she added while spinning her index finger around in the air and rolling her eyes.

Janet laughed halfheartedly and agreed. "Sure, that sounds like a plan," she said, once again pretending to smile knowing that Kirstin would never follow through with her suggestion.

People always said *Oh, let's hang out* or *We ought to have dinner soon*, but, despite the numerous proposals she received, rarely did one generate an actual invitation. She knew that Kirstin got together with several other military wives quite often, but only once had they ever invited her to one of their outings, and she'd been scheduled to work that night. She hadn't gotten an invite since, and Janet guessed they thought she'd been blowing them off or something, though she really did have to work that night.

As she watched Kirstin walk away after they said their goodbyes, Janet wondered how she kept it all together—the manicured nails, perfect hair, cute kids, bright smiles. Janet just couldn't do it. She wanted to, though. She didn't want to be miserable and sad all the time. She wanted to be the perfect little wife with a clean house to come home to every day, adorable kids who did exactly as they're told, delicious supper cooking in the oven, successful career to support the family. She was confident that she could do it all, but she hadn't figured out how to do it with a smile, and either Kirstin's smiles were all fake or she had something that Janet wanted.

After an afternoon that had been extremely wearing—both figuratively and literally in this case, considering the frustrating stains she bore—this casual run-in with a fellow army wife, who seemed to have her life all together, made Janet feel even worse about herself. Starting her ignition and backing out of the parking space, she was so glad to finally be heading home to get some much-needed relaxation.

Knowing that supper was already planned—a chicken salad sandwich and minestrone soup from the canned food shelf—was a relief because her stomach was still growling ferociously. She'd bought a pack of butter croissants from the deli, small head of lettuce, and ripe tomato to dress up the sandwich, which was rare for Janet because she didn't usually buy fresh bread or vegetables since the produce usually spoiled before she got around to eating all of it, and she hated to waste food.

*I wonder if Mr. Happy would eat my scraps now,* she pondered, hoping fiercely that he was still there.

Janet vaguely remembered those days when she and Marcus were both home every evening and what to have for dinner was actually kind of exciting, especially years ago when they were still newlyweds. Cooking dinner for her new husband was so satisfying back in those early months, and Janet had endeavored to master complex menus—stewing fresh tomatoes to make spaghetti sauce from scratch, pounding chicken breasts flat between two pieces of wax paper to roll each one up with a cheesy center, kneading dough to twist into garlic parmesan breadsticks or roll into buttermilk biscuits—before realizing that, while the way to a man's heart may be through his stomach, the complexity of what went into his mouth apparently didn't matter at all.

When she finally realized that Marcus didn't care whether he ate cream cheese-stuffed, pecan-crusted chicken breasts with twice-baked red potatoes or frozen chicken tenders and store-bought curly fries, her newlywed cooking enthusiasm came to conclusion. No matter what meal she prepared, he always told her it was good but never praised her like she wanted to be praised for coming home and spending two hours in the kitchen after a full day at work. Granted, she didn't do it for the praise; she did it to impress her new husband and show him how lucky he was. But judging by the equal way he treated the frozen, store-bought versions of her homemade dishes, her cooking didn't impress him the way she'd hoped it would.

His lack of verbal appreciation for Janet's efforts hurt her feelings, even though she tried really hard to hide it each night as she washed the mountain of dirty dishes in silence while he watched television. She knew she wasn't the greatest cook in the world, but she could follow a recipe as long as it wasn't too difficult. She sometimes took shortcuts though, and her dishes never came out as pretty as the ones in the classic red and white plaid *Better Homes and Gardens* cookbook that she loved so much. Eventually, she'd foregone homemade lasagna with made-from-scratch tomato sauce and opted instead for picking up one in the freezer section along with frozen garlic bread rather than using the bread machine they'd gotten as a wedding gift.

While they'd been going through the fertility treatments, Janet had tried to rekindle the early flame by going back to cooking most weeknights and insisting they eat in the dining room rather than in front of the television. While she didn't break out the bread machine, she did opt for fresh veggies instead of frozen ones and bread from the deli to go with her homemade lasagna made with canned tomato sauce rather than freshly stewed tomatoes. The extra communication around the dinner table boosted their relationship for a while until every conversation began to revolve around talk of babies. Tension started to run high when the subject came up, to the point that meals began to commence in silence for lack of something else to discuss. The dinners got shorter and shorter as Marcus learned to inhale food without chewing so he could escape to his recliner.

Shortly after he announced his reenlistment, Janet had stopped cooking completely. She brought home takeout or popped a frozen pizza in the oven, and the dinners together around the table had ceased. Marcus took his plate to the living room to watch television while Janet ate at the kitchen counter or standing over the sink just as she did now that he was gone. The only benefit that came out of not cooking was the quick cleanup.

Tonight, she wouldn't be eating alone though, and she was excited for once to share the evening with her new male companion, unless he'd decided to leave her too.

# Chapter 13

The smoldering heat from the engine of the truck felt as though it were burning his legs through the dusty camouflage pants. The plastic ends on the laces of his boots were nearly melting from their proximity to the engine on the floor. Marcus would never again complain of the Mississippi heat after dealing with these dreadful temperatures and baking in these non-air-conditioned trucks day after day.

On the convoy, the soldiers would ride for hours from one base to the next. In between was just desert—miles and miles of nothing but sand and a narrow little road. Roadside bombs were a constant danger, so they stuck to the center of the road whenever possible.

Marcus had seen the detonation of a few IEDs—Improvised Explosive Devices—during his previous deployment. He had witnessed a couple during this one as well but nothing like during that first deployment with Operation Iraqi Freedom. Sometimes the bomb squad, the Explosive Ordnance Disposal Specialists, that went out ahead of the convoy to sweep the road would find and safely detonate the devices in place—a very dangerous job for which Marcus was thankful some soldiers were willing to do. While he told himself to remain composed in stressful situations, Marcus was amazed at how those guys seemed downright calm as they meticulously handled deadly volatile materials.

The bomb squad did its best, but sometimes he and his fellow soldiers on the convoys weren't fortunate enough to discover the explosives in advance. These military vehicles were built to withstand a lot, but manmade equipment could only take so much. They were not indestructible, and, unfortunately, he had witnessed their destructibility firsthand.

Marcus had seen these 35,000-pound armored trucks blown several feet in the air. He'd watched them erupt instantly in wicked orange flames as shards of metal from the interior of an engine not unlike the one at his feet scorching his legs at that very moment propelled through the air like bullets from the force of the blast.

He'd helped men crawl to safety from the rubble of the damaged vehicle before it burst into flames. He'd felt a fire burn so hot that any attempt to put it out was worthless, so intense that they could only sit and watch it burn.

He'd seen men wounded.

He'd seen worse.

Man tries so hard to control everything, but fire can easily get out of man's control and destroy everything and everyone in its path. Sometimes Marcus felt that fire was similar to war in that way. Government, politicians wanted to control everything—do this, do this, do this, do this—but a government had little control, sometimes none, over what they had started, especially once they initiated war.

Sometimes a fire is just going to burn. When it reaches that point of no return, the time comes when each individual has to decide whether he will fight the flames and futilely try to put them out or plainly accept what is happening, put marshmallows on a stick, and make the best of a dire situation.

The combination of desert weather and engine heat was so hot right now, and Marcus felt he could roast marshmallows off the engine of his truck. With the way these trucks were built, the engine actually came up into the floorboard of the truck, so his leg was literally inches from the awfully hot motor. Oh, how he longed for air-conditioner and a glass of cold sweet tea!

In the South where he grew up, tea was always sweet. People didn't even say "sweet" tea in Mississippi because it was already understood. Being overseas for so long, Marcus was tired of artificial sweeteners. He wanted some real sugar in his tea, not a couple packets of Sweet-N-Low or Splenda. While he'd actually grown to slightly enjoy the bottled green tea soldiers could sometimes get, it was nothing like the South Mississippi sweet tea, especially his wife's. He used to tease her about sticking her thumb in the pitcher to make it so sweet, but it was actually more like she stubbed her toe and spilled the whole bag of sugar in there.

After unloading the grocery bags with Mr. Happy dancing around her feet begging for attention and nearly tripping her in the process, Janet was ready to relax. As she walked through the living room to the kitchen, Janet paused by the sofa to click the power button on the remote for her forty-two-inch television and scroll through the channels until stopping on a channel with music videos. It always amazed her that she paid for hundreds of channels but only watched maybe five of them.

She walked into the kitchen and grabbed a paper plate from the stack by the bread box, then popped a cup of soup in the microwave before gathering everything she needed to make her chicken salad croissant. As she spread mayonnaise on the soft bread, Janet imagined the dinner Kirstin would be preparing tonight for her two beautiful little girls—cheesy elbow macaroni and chicken tenders, traditional spaghetti and meatballs, or maybe individual pepperoni pizzas. Jealousy panged Janet's heart as she pictured the little girls helping Kirstin sprinkle mozzarella cheese over the pizza sauce and arrange pepperoni slices into smiley faces, all the while giggling and not caring about the mess they were making in the kitchen.

She sliced the tomato and placed a couple slices on top of the lettuce, then topped that with chicken before setting the croissant next to the steaming hot mug of soup she'd just set on her dinner tray. Carrying the plastic tray to the couch and walking passed Marcus's chair where she had napped yesterday afternoon with Mr. Happy, Janet felt overwhelmed with misery, a feeling she kept at bay as much as possible. Right now though, she couldn't help stopping in the middle of the living room to stare at the beige recliner as the loneliness crept up and caught in her throat.

Janet was uncertain why she never wanted to sit in his chair; it had sat empty for months until Mr. Happy plopped at its foot the day before as if insisting she sit near him. Moreover, she never even wanted to look at it, and she unconsciously averted her glance every time she walked by. However, tonight, Janet was tired of looking away. She was sick and tired of feeling this ache in her chest every time she sat down to eat dinner alone. The hollow desolation had exhausted its welcome.

On good days in years past, she would have snuggled up on his recliner with him just to get his attention. As she'd gained a few pounds over the years though, Janet had become self-conscious about sitting in his lap, even though he said he couldn't tell a difference. Those few pounds she'd acquired with age had led to sitting alone on the couch in baggy t-shirts and sweatpants while he sat across the room in his recliner. The day before he'd deployed, they'd both sat in that chair holding onto each other like they hadn't done in years, both struggling to keep back the stream of tears that wanted desperately to fall. Every time she looked at that chair, she pictured their last night together when they'd fallen asleep in that recliner, neither wanting to go to bed because they didn't want to wake and face what the next day held in store.

Janet swallowed hard, pushing the memory down deep like she'd learned to do just to get through each day's mundane activities, and sat down into Marcus's recliner instead of the couch. She rested her dinner across her lap with a sigh, then paused and smiled, imagining his irritatingly cute teasing voice making fun of her as she sighed.

Mr. Happy sat at her feet, begging for a bite of chicken salad.

"I just put a whole can of dog food in the new bowl I bought you, boy. Now, it's my turn to eat," she informed the pup, who had lain down with his nose still up in the air anticipating a treat from her plate.

Janet giggled and tossed him a tiny piece of croissant, which he swallowed whole as soon as it hit the floor.

The room looked different from Marcus's chair. Janet's gaze touched briefly on various points in the room from a perspective she wasn't certain she liked. The faux granite fireplace where they used to roast marshmallows and drink cheap merlot on budget date nights was almost completely blocked by the clutter of oversized vases filled with fake greenery she'd bought to "dress up" the room. Lately, Janet never looked at the fireplace itself, only the flat screen television mounted on the wall above it.

The dust on the base of her brushed nickel reading lamp beside the sofa, which she never noticed even though she used the lamp every day, stood out from across the room due to unnoticed swipes of hand prints. She couldn't remember the last time she'd dusted. The whole house was kept neat and tidy but not necessarily clean and spotless.

The wall of windows behind the sofa shadowed the room rather than brightened it due to the overly thick layers of curtains. She'd never noticed it before, perhaps because the curtains were behind her when she sat on the couch, but they didn't match the room at all. The outdated floral patterns of various shades of mauve plus the multiple sheer white panels cast an aged gloom over the interior of the home. She remembered choosing the mauve hue and thinking it was a colorful tone of brown, but looking at it now, the color and pattern were just bland. *Why did I want mauve? What's so special about neutral?* she thought negatively.

The curtains had to go. As soon as she finished her soup, they had to be taken down. She envisioned light beaming into the space and anticipated relaxing while looking out the windows at the trees in the backyard. With the mauve floral pattern gone, she could really decorate the room with whatever color or pattern she wanted to use since the sofa and recliner were both a neutral cocoa color.

As she pictured how different the room would look without those curtains, she thought, *Heck, why wait?* Setting her tray on the floor beside the recliner, Janet purposefully crossed the room toward the dark windows.

Standing barefooted on the cushions of the dark couch, Janet reached for the metal curtain rod with both hands, carefully lifting it from its brackets on the wall and lowering the curtains to rest on the back of the sofa. Jumping down to the floor like she'd just nailed her balance beam routine at the Olympics, she stuck her landing like a gold medalist and threw her hands in the air for the invisible audience cheering on her redecorating performance.

Janet giggled at herself before propping her hands on her hips with a sigh, the sigh making her giggle again as she realized how often she made that exasperated sound. Looking at the windows, she felt as though a tiny weight had been lifted, although, as always, work just led to more work. With the curtains gone, she could see that she really needed to wash the window panes to allow the light she had envisioned to shine through. A thick layer of grit coated the glass, embarrassing Janet, even though no one else was there to see it.

"What do you think, Mr. Happy? Think it looks better now?" she questioned the hound sitting in the middle of the room with a confused expression in his eyes. He tilted his head to one side as though considering the matter and unsure of his answer.

"Oh, what do you know about decorating, anyway? You're a man." She laughed as she scratched him on the head and tousled his ears.

After gathering the fabric to one end of the rod and slipping it off, Janet replaced the rod on its brackets and took the curtains to the laundry room before settling back down in the recliner with her dinner tray. She liked the new light, but the setting sun was steadily revealing every inch of the room that she wasn't fond of, and with each bite she saw another area of the room she'd like to change. The outdated light fixture hanging in the middle of the room, the beige carpet soiled by years of traffic, the cluttered bookcase crammed with miscellaneous paperbacks and hardbacks from Mark Twain to Danielle Steel, and the dusty floral swag hanging over the "Home Sweet Home" wall art they'd been given as a housewarming gift were visible weights Janet needed to lift.

"Humm hum hum hum," Janet began to absentmindedly sing softly a popular old Kelly Clarkson hit. "Since you've been gone, ba da da dum, I can breathe for the first time," she bobbed her head side to side to the silent beat. Her feet propped on the foot rest began tapping along to the melody in her mind as her whole body seemed to tune in to the music.

Mr. Happy picked up on her song, his tail wagging in unison with her tapping toes.

She felt a twinge of excitement, which both inspired and bothered her: inspired because she rarely got excited about anything with Marcus gone, bothered because she rarely got excited about anything with Marcus gone. It was a double-edged sword as always, but tonight she wasn't going to feel guilty for feeling happy without him, tonight she wasn't going to feel sad that he wasn't here, and tonight she wasn't going to allow the heartache to win. She was going to make some changes, and she was going to enjoy it.

"Today, I am going to smile. I am going to have fun. I am not going to worry or be sad," Janet promised herself out loud as though chanting a new mantra.

She wasn't sure why, but that song had really gotten her blood pumping, making her want to get up and do more. Removing the curtains just wasn't enough. She put her paper plate in the trash and her soup bowl in the sink and came back into the living room looking at it through fresh eyes as though she'd never seen it before

"Time to get to work, Mr. Happy."

Surveying the room, Janet stared at the couch, which sat facing the window at a ninety-degree angle from the fireplace. The recliner was sitting opposite the couch, and the right side of the room was open to the dining room. Years ago, Janet had arranged the furniture like this so traffic could flow.

As she stood there staring at the couch with her hands on her hips, she wondered why traffic flow had ever even crossed her mind since there was no traffic. It wasn't like this was a busy road. This was a one-person street, so flow of traffic really didn't matter.

Deciding to move the couch away from the window, Janet grabbed the right arm of the sofa and then began to push and heave and hoe and pull the couch away from the wall, not daring to peek at the mess underneath that was revealed when she moved it. She wasn't sure exactly where she wanted to move the couch, but she knew she wanted to see out the window without any obstruction. She wanted to look outside to the backyard, to that big oak tree. She'd never been able to see it from inside the house, and it added a little touch of Marcus. She could see the swing and faintly see the initials carved on its bark.

*Who said a couch has to be pushed up against a wall?* Janet wondered.

She could move the couch to the wall opposite where it had sat for years in the open area to divide the dining room and living area. Getting it there was going to be a task, so she pushed one side of the couch forward a few inches then moved to the other side and repeated the motion, almost as though it were a dance. She pushed and switched sides as though she were doing a waltz. She added a little step ball change.

*Push, pull, step ball change sides.*
*Push, pull, step ball change sides.*
*Push, pull, step ball change sides.*

Mr. Happy darted around the room, not sure where to hide from the big piece of furniture being pushed around.

"Don't hide! I'm not going to bother you!" Janet exclaimed as Mr. Happy began to retreat to the kitchen to avoid being run over.

A new high tempo song started blasting through the speakers. Push, step, push, step, she moved her feet and the couch in double time trying to keep up with the beat of the music.

Resting against the arm of the couch and observing the new layout, she still wasn't quite satisfied. Unsure whether or not she liked the new arrangement with the sofa angled away from the corner, Janet marched a couple circles around the couch, realizing that she could see a lot of bruises in the future for her klutzy self because it was a fairly long couch with little space on either side. She couldn't push it up against either of those walls because that cut off her own flow of traffic.

*Maybe the couch should go where the recliner is, facing the fireplace?* She pictured it in her mind, and then started the dance over again.

*Push, pull, step ball change sides.*
*Push, pull, step ball change sides.*
*Push, pul,l step ball change sides.*

She liked the new arrangement. She had to pause to move the recliner out of the way, not sure where it was going to go. She didn't want it sitting in front of the window, so that really only left one option. The recliner definitely couldn't sit in front of the window where she'd moved it temporarily because it would block her view. With the fireplace and couch in position, that only left one option. So she moved the chair to the open side of the room and angled it slightly toward the television, back to the dining room.

*If Marcus were here, he would hate this,* she considered. He hated moving furniture. Actually, it seemed he hated it when she did anything that required assistance from him. He told her after the last piece of furniture he'd bought that she wasn't allowed to buy any more because he wasn't moving another thing. That's okay, she thought. There were some things she didn't need him for. Like the little red hen, she could do it herself.

It was actually kind of fun, surprisingly. With the couch against the new wall, she plopped down on the center cushion to see how she liked it. From there, she had a perfect view of the oak tree through the window, straight view of the flat screen television and stone fire place, which was no longer blocked.

She didn't like the coffee table; it was a little too formal for her true tastes. She would donate it to a local mission if her sister didn't want it; her sister liked decorous things.

"Mr. Happy? Where'd you go?"

The floppy ears bounced as the pup bounded into the room and jumped on her lap before she could stop him. "Well, at least somebody loves me," she said with a slight laugh.

Janet picked up the remote control from the seat cushion beside her and clicked the button to change the channel to a romantic movie on one of the channels she only got to watch now that Marcus was gone. She stretched her legs across the cushions and let Mr. Happy snuggle up to her chest. He sighed heavily, and she smiled as she felt his whole body relax against her.

The handsome man on the television with the Superman-esque square jaw placed his hands on the face of the heroine and professed his love for her, looking passionately into her eyes and wiping away a single tear from her cheek with his thumb. Janet's heart skipped a beat at the unrealistic scene, feeling the woman's excitement as her own. A sucker for romance, Janet wished she had some in her own life, but Hallmark movies were as close as she could get.

# Chapter 14

The key lime pie on her tray wasn't as good as the banana pudding she'd wanted earlier that week, but it was a close second best dessert from the nursing home kitchen. Janet really didn't feel like eating in the nurse's lounge or the crowded cafeteria, so she carried her tray outside to the terrace to enjoy the garden view and fresh air, which were a happy accompaniment for any meal. Janet had the terrace to herself. She took a small bite of her meatloaf, savoring the mixture of flavors on her tongue. The kitchen had the some of the best meatloaf Janet had ever tried, definitely not characteristic of the bland food most people would expect from a hospital-type environment, although the homemade mashed potatoes could definitely use some salt and butter.

She enjoyed her meal in relative silence, allowing her mind to clear for a while before going back to her afternoon routine. As she admired the garden, a wheelchair peaked around the corner of the pathway and turned in her direction. She smiled and lifted her hand in a small wave as Russ approached pushing his mom back toward the terrace doors.

Janet admired the breadth of the man's shoulders as he bent over to hug the elderly woman. She could envision the muscles of his back and pictured him more naturally in a t-shirt rather than the navy blazer he wore.

"I'll be there in a few minutes, Mom," he said with his gaze intent on Janet sitting at the table alone. Janet thought she saw the old woman smiled as the nurse wheeled her inside, and Janet found herself face to face with the same man who'd captivated her attention too often lately.

He walked slowly toward her without saying a word until he was standing right next to her table, his broad form shadowing the tray sitting in front of her.

"We have to stop meeting like this," he smiled, the depth of his voice penetrating something deep in Janet's gut. Without waiting for an invitation from her, he pulled out a chair and sat down beside her.

Janet had been around handsome men before—her husband for one—but this man with his chiseled jaw and thick chest belonged shirtless on the cover of a romance novel rescuing a damsel in distress or dressed in tights and a cape saving the world in a comic book. His mere presence triggered goose bumps on Janet's skin.

"I was hoping I'd run into you here," he said. Janet studied her mashed potatoes intently, not daring to look up at Russ's blue eyes.

"How long have you worked here?" he questioned, obviously with no intentions of letting her spend her lunch break in peaceful silence.

"A while," she answered noncommittally, brushing her hair from in front of her face and tucking it behind her ear nervously.

Why this gorgeous man would be paying her so much attention, Janet had no idea. She shifted in her chair, feeling both excited and uncomfortable at the same time. She'd thought about him so often since the restaurant that she had almost convinced herself that he was imaginary.

But the man at her table was real, and he was smiling at her revealing his perfectly white teeth that could only belong to a Colgate commercial. *How can one man be really this good-looking?* she wondered.

"You really make scrubs look beautiful. Do you know that?" he asked.

Janet smiled involuntarily but rolled her eyes at his obvious attempt at flirting, although she still couldn't imagine why someone like him would be flirting with someone like her.

"What was that for?" he grinned, referring to the way she rolled her eyes.

Janet cleared her throat and looked him square in the eye, preparing to put him in his place. "You know I'm married. You shouldn't be complimenting me like that."

Russ looked her square in the eyes with a serious expression. "You should be told every day that you are beautiful, and he is obviously not here to tell you that every day like you deserve."

Janet bit her bottom lip, hating that he made her feel so confused. "He had to go. It's not his fault," she defended Marcus although she didn't believe her own words.

"You don't believe that," he said softly, reading her true thoughts with ease. "If you ever do decide you're ready to admit the truth, I'll be here to listen."

On that note, he pushed back his chair and stood to leave. Janet's bottom lip hurt from trying to keep her thoughts to herself. Part of her wanted to call him back and spill her whole life story to this man she barely knew, but she couldn't talk about her husband and their problems to Russ.

She had to deal with this on her own.

Stepping through the double doors of the auditorium onto the planked floor later that evening, Janet wiped her sweaty palms on her pleated navy skirt. Her nerves had been on high alert all afternoon since her lunchtime encounter with the handsome stranger named Russ. She didn't know why her gut had such a strong reaction to seeing him again, but she didn't like it.

Her discomfort only enhanced the extent that she always felt out of place at these military spouse events, although she'd never fully understood why anxiety got the best of her considering all the women there were in the same situation as herself. Their husbands were all deployed, most to the same base in the middle of hostile territory, and outsiders would probably assume this common concern would instigate instant camaraderie among the women. But it didn't.

Janet felt as though she were in high school again when she'd spent an hour each morning wondering what to wear so the cool girls wouldn't laugh at her. Her frizzy, unruly hair and metal mouth had left her feeling self-conscious back then, and the spoiled brats she went to school with didn't help matters much. She'd learned in junior high that girls could be really mean when she'd worn what she thought was a cute top and been teased because it wasn't a name brand. It didn't take many instances like that before a young Janet had quit trying to be cool and fit in. She'd rather be an outsider by choice than by rejection.

Janet never outgrew that outsider mindset, which made her situation now, fifteen years after that first taunting, even more difficult. She wanted, no, she *needed* friends to help her through this deployment, but she couldn't seem to let her guard down and put herself out there for fear of rejection.

Rejection was definitely not the vibe she'd gotten from Russ at either of their incidental meetings.

Looking for a place to sit at this Family Readiness Group gathering was like high school lunchtime during which Janet had often chosen to skip lunch and sit in the library or computer lab until the next class began. In her senior year, when her classmates had all gone off campus together for lunch, Janet had gotten food from a drive-through and parked her car in a secluded spot to eat alone. No one ever even asked where she'd been when they all returned to campus; they never even noticed or cared that she wasn't with the rest of the class.

As Janet scanned the room for a safe seat, she made eye contact with Kirstin who had turned to look toward the door, flipping her blonde hair over her shoulder as she shifted in her chair. Her face lit up, and she began waving for Janet to come over to her table. Janet smiled genuinely knowing the evening would pass a lot quicker with Kristin to keep conversation flowing. She didn't understand why someone like Kirstin would want to be friends with someone like her. Kirstin was one of the cool kids, and Janet wasn't.

As Janet made her way across the room, she noticed that every woman there wore a smile, which was completely unrealistic with a group of women this large. She imagined the reasons for their smiles as she passed each one. Some were genuinely happy people 24/7, and Janet envied them. Others were in high spirits to simply have a babysitter and get a night off from the kids. Some smiles were obviously practiced, like Janet's often was, rehearsed for months to avoid those "Aw, you poor lonely thing" glances from relatives. Some were habitual, formed through years of doing what they were supposed to do so much that it now became second nature. Others were clearly faked, accompanied by rolling eyes and exasperated sighs.

The ladies at Kirstin's table all greeted Janet politely as she pulled out a seat to join them. Polite chitchat ensued as more and more people began to take their seats.

At exactly six thirty in the evening, the Family Readiness Group president walked to the podium, smoothing her pastel yellow business suit with her palms. "Well, ladies, I'd like to welcome you to this FRG-sponsored event. We're so glad y'all could join us today for some fun and fellowship," she said with her southern drawl. She introduced herself and told a little of her military affiliation then led right into the program. "Today we're gonna put together some care packages for our deployed soldiers with items donated by local organizations. But first, before we get started, please stand as we pledge allegiance to the flag and then remain standing for our national anthem, which will be sung by Mrs. Bonnie Faye."

The women all stood and placed their hands over their hearts in salute to the flag their husbands were defending, and they remained standing quietly as the national anthem was sung before returning to their seats. The FRG president returned to the podium as the women all sat back down.

"I'd like to thank the following businesses for their support of our troops and their military families: First Baptist Church for the Bible Study books, First National Bank for the click pens, Main Street Pharmacy for eyedrops and Chap Stick, Mama's Lil' Bakery for chocolate chip cookies, Greene's Grocery for a variety of canned meats, The Mississippi Coast Journal for current copies of the newspaper, Hot 102.5 FM for CDs, Books-n-Stuff for puzzle booklets, Video Market for assorted DVDs, and Whaley's Office Supply for packing materials. Let's give all of these businesses a big round of applause."

The women all clapped as they were instructed, and Janet looked around the table at the items donated by the business just listed.

"At this time, I'd like to welcome Chaplain Smith who will be giving a short devotion before we begin our care packages. Chaplain," she said, holding out her hand and offering the podium to the man in uniform.

"Thank you for allowing me the opportunity to be here tonight," he began. "'1 Thessalonians 5:18 states, 'In every thing give thanks: for this is the will of God in Christ Jesus concerning you.' Please join me now in a prayer of thanks," he said, bowing his head.

"Dear Lord, we thank you for your wonderful love and unfailing mercy. We praise you for the many blessings you bestow on us every day. I thank you for these faithful women and for the sacrifices they make daily for our country. Lord, please bless these women and their families. Give them the strength they need to get through each day of this deployment, and constantly remind them that they are never alone, that you are always with them in every situation. In the name of your son Jesus, Amen.

"Today, I want all of you spectacular ladies to know one thing," he said holding his right index finger up in the air and pausing. "You are not alone. Feeling loneliness is normal when your spouse is away for so long, but no matter how lonely you feel, you are not alone," he pointed around the room from table to table.

"Many of you are mothers who face the challenges of managing a household essentially as a single parent while your husband is away. You may feel at times that you have to do everything on your own, without help. I urge you to heed the words of Psalm 37:5, 'Commit thy way unto the LORD; trust also in him; and he shall bring it to pass.' God will help you, and you, and you," he pointed to various women throughout the auditorium. "You are not alone.

"Others of you who have no children may find yourself going home each day to an empty house, and the loneliness can drag you down. But, ladies, you are never alone. James tells us in chapter 4 verse 8, 'Draw nigh to God and he will draw nigh to you.' God wants to draw you close, to hold you when you're lonely. You are not alone.

"I appreciate your sacrifices for this great country, and so do your families. We understand that being a military spouse is not easy, and there will be times when you'll need assistance. Please know that the army has assistance available in the form of counseling, and we would be glad to help you in any way we can.

If you'd like more information about these services, please visit one of the tables in the lobby before you leave.

"I'll leave you with Paul's words in Romans chapter five, 'And not only so, but we glory in tribulations also: knowing that tribulation worketh patience; and patience, experience; and experience, hope.' Everything you are enduring now is helping to mold you into the woman, the mother, the wife, the friend that God wants you to be."

"Ugh," Janet sighed. This upbeat mumbo jumbo always just made her feel worse about herself rather than better.

"What's wrong?" Kirstin whispered.

"Nothing. Just how in the world can someone rejoice in suffering? What am I supposed to do—be happy that my husband is gone?" Janet complained.

Kirstin shook her head lightly and smiled understandingly. "The verse says *in*, not *about*. He isn't saying 'be happy *about* your suffering.' He means rejoice or praise God in the midst of it. In the middle of our problems, we should still be thankful that God can use every circumstance for his good," she explained. "No matter how hard it becomes." She sat quietly for a few moments before excusing herself to the ladies room, leaving Janet and the other women at the table to begin sorting though the items on the table.

Janet thought about Kirstin's explanation of the verse and knew it made a lot more sense the way she phrased it than the way Janet had perceived it.

The women chatted about menial things as they packed the boxes full of donations to send to their husbands' units. At least three units were represented at this one event, and the boxes would be divided among all of them.

After about fifteen minutes of separating cans of Spam among the boxes at her table, Janet noticed that Kirstin had not returned, and she excused herself to go check on the other woman, concerned that something was wrong from the uncharacteristic way Kirstin had slipped quietly away.

She slipped through the crowd to the doors at the back of the auditorium and followed the hallway to the ladies' room.

Opening the door quietly, Janet observed Kirstin's teary-eyed reflection in the long mirror. Kirstin was talking to herself—she thought she heard her saying something about shaking—and dabbing her cheeks with a tissue when she saw Janet standing in the doorway.

The two women stared at each other in the mirror, sharing a moment of quiet understanding. Janet crossed the room toward her friend and, without saying a word, wrapped her arms around the crying woman's shoulders. Kirstin sobbed softly onto Janet's shoulder for several minutes before lifting her head with a final sniffle and pulling away.

Janet stood beside her, both facing the mirror, as Kirstin smoothed concealer beneath her eyes and touched up the powder on her cheeks.

"Thanks," she whispered to Janet, and Janet nodded.

"Are you okay?"

"Most days," Kirstin smiled. "Sometimes it hits harder in others...you know?"

Janet knew. She didn't need to know exactly what had triggered Kirstin's laments to understand the sentiments.

The pair walked out of the ladies' room together, holding hands as they walked down the hallway. Kirstin paused to take a deep breath then gave Janet's hand a squeeze before she released it as they reached the doors to the auditorium and walked in to rejoin the crowd.

Kirstin's tears evoked a mixed response within Janet as they took their seats. No one at the table would suspect from her smooth complexion that she'd just been crying in the bathroom. Were it Janet the one in tears, she'd been too blotchy for a little concealer and powder to fix.

Janet sympathized with the other woman for whatever had upset her, yet the part of her that had envied Kirstin for having a seemingly perfect life experienced something resembling relief. She would never wish bad fortune on a friend and like seeing Kirstin distressed, but Janet felt better about her own sadness, her own failure to control her emotions after witnessing the other woman's moment of weakness.

The ladies all laughed at something Kirstin had just said, and Janet laughed along, even though she hadn't been paying attention to the conversation and had no idea what was supposed to be so funny. Kirstin's cheeks were flushed as she continued her funny story—something about her twins trying on her high heels—and, from the way the woman was smiling, Janet could no longer determine if the flush on her cheeks was caused by crying or laughing.

Kirstin may not have her life all together perfectly like Janet had believed, but she had something Janet wanted—the ability to laugh when she wanted to cry. Where that inner strength came from, Janet wasn't one hundred percent certain, but she had a pretty good idea.

With the boxes all packed and ready to ship, the women began to file out of the auditorium into the parking lot. Noticing Kirstin gathering her things, Janet lingered behind those who rushed out the doors first to get a moment alone to talk to Kirstin.

"You feeling any better?" she asked as Kirstin tucked her cell phone in her purse.

"I'm fine. The chaplain just said a few things that struck me pretty hard, I guess."

"I know what you mean. That's why I don't really like going to church anymore," Janet admitted, shrugging her shoulders.

"But church is where you need to be most," Kirstin asserted, looking a little surprised by Janet's statement about not attending church. "This deployment is hard, but I can't imagine going through it without relying on God for my strength. He's the only reason I can get up every morning with a smile lots of days."

Janet nodded her head slightly. "So that's your secret, huh? I've wondered how you could be so happy all the time when I'm absolutely miserable when I go home most days."

"It's not a secret. It's a fact I'll gladly tell anyone," the blonde woman declared as she picked up her purse and put the strap over her shoulder. "'Truly he is my rock and my salvation; he is my fortress, I will not be shaken,'" she quoted with a bright smile.

"I will not be shaken," Janet repeated. "Is that what you were saying to yourself in the bathroom when I walked in?"

"Yep," Kirstin admitted, tilting her head to one side and raising her shoulders. "You caught me. Psalm 62. I repeat it when I start feeling upset to remind myself that nothing can shake my foundation when I'm standing on the solid rock. Helps me to remember that every day."

The two women said their goodbyes and went their separate ways in the parking lot, but Kirstin's words stayed with Janet the whole ride home, much like her own mother's declaration days before that things would soon be getting better. Maybe they finally were.

# Chapter 15

The tree top rustled lightly from the breeze, which carried the heat of the late summer evening making Janet cherish one of the last few evenings she could spend outside with Mr. Happy before the bad weather could set in.

The pair lazily sat in the wooden swing in the backyard. Janet's bare feet grazed the tall blades of uncut grass with each glide of the swing back and forth.

She hadn't cut the grass in a couple of weeks. That chore was definitely one Janet would gladly hand back over to Marcus once he got home. Mr. Happy would be glad for the grass to get cut too. For a stray pup that had been eating garbage a week ago, he had sure become spoiled in a hurry, tiptoeing across the grass and always following the concrete or stone path rather than cutting across the yard. Little fellow hated his paws getting wet or dirty.

A pair of redbirds flew overhead, lighting briefly on the branches of the old oak before fluttering off around the yard.

The sprinkler hose woven through the flower bed made a hissing sound as the water sprayed the recently planted flowers.

Janet patted Mr. Happy on his blonde head, which was laid across her thigh. *Spoiled rotten,* she thought with a grin. Very appropriately named, Mr. Happy had quickly become the highlight of Janet's days.

As she stroked his floppy ears with one hand, Janet aimlessly tapped the eraser of her pencil against the white legal pad in her lap thinking of how to begin her letter to Marcus. She wanted to tell him about how cute Mr. Happy was with his head resting on her lap and how he greeted her at the door when she got home each afternoon.

> *Dear Marcus,*
>
> *Where do I begin? Work is work, as always. My patients ask about you every day, and I tell them you're doing fine. I hope that's true, that you are doing fine.*

She paused, pencil tapping monotonously on the paper again.

> *I'm sorry I don't ask more questions about how you're doing when we talk. I guess I figure you'll tell me what you want me to know whether I ask or not. If it comes across as though I don't care, that's not true. I do care. Honestly. I guess I just don't want to ask how you're doing and hear you say something is wrong.*

Janet felt guilty for not being more supportive of Marcus. He was at war, yet she was the one who needed encouragement.

That was how it always was when he was home. Marcus had always been the encourager of the family, the one to look for the bright side of the situation while Janet was the practical one. There wasn't always a bright side; sometimes, you just did what you had to do to get things done.

*I bet you get tired of hearing me list everything that's wrong. Don't you? But lately, nothing seems to be right. Lately it seems like everything is falling apart, and I don't know how much longer I can hold it together by myself.*

Janet's jaw tightened as she tried to squeeze back a tear that was threatening to fall.

*I'm ready for this to be over. I'm ready for this part of our lives to be done...*

She barely heard the vibration of the phone ringing from where it lay on the grass under the swing. She grabbed the phone and swung her feet to the grass all in the same motion.

She drew pictures, squiggly lines in the grass, dragging her toe across the blades in shapes and circles and lines. Marcus always teased her how she couldn't be still when she talked on the phone, had to be up and moving around. She'd read online somewhere that suggested you should clean the house while you talk on the phone—dust your furniture with one hand while you talk with the other, or clean your bathroom mirrors or windows while you chatted. She'd never really been able to do anything productive like that while she was on the phone; she just walked around, paced back and forth, walked in circles from one room to the next. Her nervous energy wouldn't let her be still.

"Hello?" she answered as she gathered her things and walked to the backdoor of the house.

"Hey, Janet! What's up?" her sister asked from the other end of the line.

"Not much, just sitting outside on the swing."

"You sound tired. I tried to call you earlier, but you didn't answer."

Janet looked at her phone and saw the icon showing she had two missed calls. "Sorry, I was at an FRG meeting and haven't looked at my phone since I left."

"It's all right. What are you doing this weekend?" Julia asked her sister.

"Nothing, I guess. I need to wash clothes and clean the house. Got some stuff I should do around here while I'm off work."

"Well, I was going to take Lucy to the movies Saturday afternoon and wondered if you want to tag along," Julia offered.

Janet rolled her eyes. She genuinely appreciated her sister's invitation but despised the phrase "tag along." She detested that her role nowadays was just to tag along. She never felt like part of the group. She was just the extra person they felt sorry for. Why couldn't Julia just say, "Hey! Would you like to go with Lucy and me to the movies?" No, she had to say "tag along."

Tag is a game kids play when they are six years old. That and red rover. Janet didn't feel like playing any games, and she wanted to be treated like she was important, not some afterthought who had to tag along.

"What time are you guys leaving?" Janet asked, accepting that any invitation was better than none at all.

"Well, we're going to the matinee because it's supposed to start raining that night. If you can't go, I understand."

Of course, her sister never asked what was convenient for Janet. Every invitation from her was from a this-is-what's-happening-tag-along-if-you-want kind of attitude. Janet simply wanted to be asked, "Hey would you like to go to the movies? What time's good for you? We were hoping to go to a matinee, but we're flexible. Are there any movies you'd like to see?" Nope. It was always, "Hey, we're going at three o'clock. You can go or not, doesn't matter," making her feel like her presence really wasn't desired, and pity was the only reason she was even being asked in the first place.

Her sister may not have meant it to sound that way, and Janet knew she was overly sensitive because of how she viewed herself. She felt unimportant, so she expected people to treat her like she was unimportant. She felt like no one genuinely cared, so she expected to be treated as if they didn't care. It was a lose-lose situation. She didn't know if she felt that way because they treated her that way, or if she was just imagining being treated that way because she felt that way. She wasn't sure where the circle began and ended, but that was how she felt, nevertheless.

"Yeah, I guess three o'clock will be fine," she answered. "I don't really have anything else going on, so it shouldn't be a big deal."

"Okay, well, I'll see you later I guess," she said.

"All right, well, what movie are we going to see?" Janet asked before her sister hurried off the phone. Janet expected it to be some stupid cartoon, and she really disliked cartoons. Kids were cute, but she didn't like going to see something that was meant for children.

Cartoons fascinated Marcus. Where most grown men had a collection of action movies on DVD, Marcus had a collection of cartoons from *Bambi* to *Lilo and Stitch*, and he was always quoting lines from the cartoons. Sometimes his funny voiceovers made her laugh, but most of the time she just rolled her eyes and wished he'd act like a grown-up.

Now that he was gone, she realized that after rolling her eyes she usually did smile at his childish antics. Without his playful demeanor around, she rarely ever smiled while she sat at home by herself until the past week with Mr. Happy around.

Mr. Happy had jumped onto the couch when they'd walked inside, claiming the cushion on the far side and had waited for Janet to sit down beside him before laying his head down and going to sleep. She had obviously stayed out past his bedtime tonight.

"Oh, you know, Lucy wants to see that new Pixar film about the princess," Julia said.

"Okay. You just want me to meet you guys there?" Janet asked.

"That's fine, we'll see you there a little before three on Saturday."

They said their goodbyes.

Janet didn't realize how worried her family was about her. They knew she sat at home all the time and worried about her well-being. Depression was their fear. It was serious, and they didn't really know how to get her out of that funk. When Marcus had been home, she'd spent most of her time with him, not as much with them, so they didn't know her attitude well enough to know how to fix it, which is pretty sad, but that's life. How well do most families know each other? Janet knew that they had good intentions. She could tell they were concerned, but the way they went about helping sometimes just ticked her off. It made her angry that her life had become everyone's pity. She didn't know what to do about it. She didn't want to be sad like this. She didn't want everyone's pity. She didn't want people to think she was miserable, but she was and she hated it. She didn't know how to fix it.

She rolled her head around, stretching her neck clockwise in a circle then back around counterclockwise and then shook her arms like she was shaking off those thoughts.

Staring at the muted television she'd accidently forgotten to switch off when she went to the FRG meeting, she saw the dancers on the video and thought how they seemed to be trapped in the screen with no music. Janet related to them because her daily routine for so long had no beat, no pulse, as though someone had just clicked the mute button and simply left her there trapped in a box.

She used to think that Marcus was her pulse, the reason her heart kept beating, but she was beginning to realize that her relationship with him wasn't the root of her heartache. Her distress was deeper.

Janet shook her head. She didn't want to be a frantic dancer stuck in a box jerking around to no music.

She changed the television channel and settled in on the couch cushions, Mr. Happy looking at her sleepily from his spot at her feet.

"I know you're ready for bed, boy. Just thirty more minutes, okay? Then we'll go to bed."

He laid his head down, disappointedly resigning to being kept awake a little longer as Janet tried to relax after her long evening.

He had been tired before, worn-out and exhausted, but this was different.

His eyes burned viciously; they just wouldn't close. His lids weren't drooping, the area beneath his eyes wasn't puffy, but his eyes burned so badly from dryness and sleeplessness that he hardly dared to blink for fear of making it worse.

He had passed the point of yawning and nodding off to sleep throughout the day and assumed he must have reached a state of delirium. Night runs under the protection of darkness, the strain of being constantly alert and on the lookout for enemy attacks and the distress from being away from home all attributed to his dilemma, but Marcus couldn't pinpoint what had changed to make him this way. He'd handled all of those things well for months.

Although a soldier's stress level is expected to be higher than that of most average citizens, Marcus didn't feel stressed. On the contrary, having forgotten what stress itself felt like because it had become his norm, Marcus felt blank.

At some point, he had foregone noticing the effects of stress on his body and mind, and he had accepted his state as normal. He never felt *stressed*; he just felt the same way he did every other day, no longer able to make the distinction between life with or without stress. Life was just life, and stress was a given part of it.

As Janet would say, his nerves were shot. Marcus recalled her saying that phrase on a regular basis when he asked what was wrong after she had come home from work and sat around watching television without a word. He wondered if this was how she had felt when she said that, if she'd been simply going through the motions because she felt numb.

If so, he kicked himself mentally for letting her go on that way for months and blamed himself. He knew now what life was like to go through the motions out of necessity because one didn't feel the desire or energy to do anything else. He ate out of habit, showered out of habit, dressed out of habit and would even lie down out of habit, but he couldn't close his eyes.

Most nights, Marcus just laid his head on his pillow until morning. He was certain that at some point each night he probably did drift off, yet barely long enough to keep him functioning in the most basic ways.

Laughter was too much of an effort. He didn't have the energy to muster a smile much of the time, which was nothing like the guy who drew attention at every family gathering with his humorous gags and teasing.

He still did his duties, went to his workouts, did everything that was expected of him, yet his sense of feeling had ceased, and he desperately wanted it back.

He wanted to be the man she had married, a man she trusted and admired. He wanted to earn her love again and hoped he wasn't too late.

The one benefit from not being able to sleep during the early hours of the morning was that he could call Janet hopefully before she went to sleep. Five in the morning for him was late in the evening for her, perfect timing as she would probably be going to bed around the time.

He opened his computer and pulled up the Skype window. After making sure his webcam was on, he clicked her picture to make the call.

On the other end, thousands of miles away, the ring of her laptop startled Janet's drift off into slumber. She quickly sat up on the couch, fluffed her hair around then patted her cheeks hoping she didn't look like a total mess before clicking "answer" on her screen. They only saw each other once every couple of weeks online, so she didn't want to look like a mess.

Marcus was staring at the ceiling blinking heavily when his picture came to view on Janet's computer.

"Hi," she said groggily.

"Hey, beautiful," he answered.

They talked back and forth about the usual topics of their daily routines while Janet fought off yawn after yawn, hoping he didn't notice. The conversation lulled for a moment as Marcus's expression turned serious.

"You look tired," he said.

"I'm sorry," she responded defensively.

"Don't be sorry. I'm just making an observation," he paused. "You look different, that's all."

"I am different," Janet said. "And I'm tired of being miserable. I'm tired of being sad and tired all the time."

"Things are going to be better once I get home," Marcus said. "I don't want you to be sad. I love you, and I want to make you happy."

Neither of them spoke as Janet took a deep breath trying to keep calm, but her sleepiness and frustration poured out.

"If you want to make me happy, then why did you reenlist? Huh?" she asked angrily. "You knew I didn't want you to. You knew. We'd talked about it over and over again before, and you'd said that you weren't going to, that we were going to start a family."

"But we didn't start a family," he said, his own frustrations starting to show through his clenched teeth. "We tried. But it didn't work."

"So your solution was to just give up on me? Where was your faith? Is that what you do? Be tough but then give up when things seem bleak? You have no idea how hard it was for me to do those injections over and over and over again, but I did them every day so we could have the family we always talked about. And after all that I'd put my body through, you gave up. You just gave up and ran off to play soldier and left me here alone. I told you I didn't want to do this again, that I didn't want to go through a second deployment, and you didn't care."

Janet threw her hands up gesturing at the computer screen.

Marcus raised his voice, "I did care!"

While Janet shook her head in disbelief, his voice lowered to a whisper as he mumbled, "I always cared, but I just couldn't handle it anymore. I couldn't be strong about it. I'd had all I could take of failing. I'm a failure."

Janet swallowed hard, unsure how to respond to his admission. "Why didn't you tell me you felt like that?" she asked quietly. "Why didn't you tell me you wanted to stop treatments? We could've talked about it. We had other options. You didn't have to go sign up without my consent and run off to the desert for a year."

The silence lingered between them as Marcus rubbed his temples and Janet waited.

"I didn't know what else to do," he said. "I felt like I needed to get away from the whole situation."

"You mean, you needed to get away from me."

"I didn't know how to face you and tell you that I couldn't do it anymore. So yeah, I ran away. I guess I did take the easy way out," he answered back.

"You know, Marcus, it's sad that you consider going to war the easy way out," Janet sighed. "All you had to do was talk to me, all you had to do was talk to me."

"I'm sorry."

"Me, too. But sorry doesn't bring you home."

"No, it doesn't."

"So what do we do now?" she asked.

Marcus shrugged, "I don't know. I don't want to go through those treatments again when I get home, but I know you still want a family, don't you?

"Yeah, I do. Maybe when you get home, we can talk about other options, discuss other avenues. There are lots of little kids out there who need good parents."

"Yeah, but I don't know how I feel about adoption. I always wanted a kid of my own. Plus won't adoption take a couple more years? I'll be an old man by the time the kid graduates if we wait a few more years."

"Well, I feel like I've spent half our marriage waiting for something else. When we first got married, it wasn't long before you deployed then I spent a year waiting for you to come home. Then we had a few really good years, but then we decided to start a family. So I spent a couple of years waiting for that to happen until you announced you were leaving. Then you left, and I've been waiting for you to come home ever since. If it's the Lord's plan for me to have to wait a couple more years, then I guess I have no other choice. I guess that's what I'll have to do. But if it's his plan for me to wait another couple of years then it not work out again, I don't know if I can handle that," Janet admitted.

"I'm not saying no. I'm just saying we need to think about it. That's a really big decision, something we don't need to jump into. We need to wait until I get home in a few months and talk about it then, but I just don't know if I can raise someone else's child as my own," Marcus said sternly.

Janet tried to disguise her frown with a yawn, conceding to the fact that he was putting the subject off again.

"Okay." She nodded, accepting the end of the discussion for the time being.

They talked a few more minutes about menial things, but the conversation remained at the forefront of each of their minds until they said their goodbyes and promised to talk again soon, each lost in his or her own thoughts as they closed the chat windows on their laptops, one to get ready for bed and the other to get ready for breakfast.

# Chapter 16

The rest of Janet's work week passed as usual without anything new other than cooler temperatures, and Janet's plans for Saturday consisted of purple polka-dotted pajamas, fuzzy slippers, and made-for-television movies turned up loud to block out the sound of approaching thunder. Cozying up on the couch with the newly spoiled hound and her laptop, she planned to spend her Friday evening browsing the newsfeeds on her social networking sites, reading people's statuses about prepping for the storm and laughing at funny cartoons her online friends had shared over the last several days.

Concerned about the imminent storm, Janet had stopped by the store on her way home from work to pick up a few survival necessities but had ended up buying a new pair of heels instead, along with a colorful scarf and matching gloves while she was there. Upon arriving home, she'd let in Mr. Happy, plunked the bags and her purse down on the kitchen counter, poured a glass of tea and kicked off her shoes before walking sock-footed into the living room.

She caught the first few minutes of the news, listening to updates on the impending storm, before changing the television channel to something more pleasant.

Janet knew her neighborhood should be safe from flooding, but the predicted high winds concerned her because hundred-year-old trees lined the streets and towered in yards throughout her neighborhood, including her own. The wind had been whipping in strong gusts since she'd pushed her shopping cart through the parking lot at the department store, blowing unattended carts across the rows into parked cars.

Her laptop dinged and displayed a new message in the chat box at the corner of her computer screen.

*U haven't blown away yet, have you?* the message asked.

The corners of her lips unconsciously curved upward as she recognized the sender.

*I don't think so. Still here,* she typed back, shrugging her shoulders as though the gesture could be seen through the text. *How'd you find me?*

Janet paused, not realizing she was biting her lower lip waiting to see how the handsome stranger who recently kept crossing her path would respond.

*I'm magic,* he wrote, followed by a winking face emoticon.

Apparently not wanting to sound like a stalker, he added, *Not many Janets work @Springing Hills. Simple deduction.*

*Oh.* Janet wasn't sure what else to say to him.

*R u ready 4 the storm?* he asked. *Sounds like its going 2 b really rough.*

*I guess so. Got some batteries and candles today just in case,* she answered, really wishing he would type in normal language rather than using text jargon. Janet would never understand why a grown, educated adult would want to give the impression of a lazy teenager who was failing language arts. Picturing this handsome, masculine, obviously successful man sitting at a computer, probably pecking away at the keyboard with only his pointer fingers, typing "ur" instead of "your" and "2" instead of "to" made her shake her head and roll her eyes.

*Did u think 2 buy bottled water? The shelves were almost empty @ the grocery store when I was there @ lunch.*

Janet shook her head as she typed, *Nope. Didn't think about that. Oh well, I'm not going back outside now in this weather.* Looking through the sliding glass door in the living room, Janet shuttered at the sight of the limbs of the lofty oak in her backyard swaying threateningly low under the force of the wind.

*I can bring u some if u want me 2. I wouldn't wanna think u were out in this weather,* he typed, showing his concern.

*Thanks, but I'll be fine.*

*What are your plans for tomorrow?* Russ asked.

*Absolutely nothing!* Janet replied with a closed-lip smile, breathing in deeply through her nose and exhaling dramatically, emphasizing her need for a day off.

*U don't work on the wknd?*

*Sometimes, but not usually,* she answered, a schoolgirl nervousness beating unsteadily in her chest.

*So u spend most wknds @ home by urself?* Russ pried.

She paused to contemplate how to respond. Janet knew that his interest was more than friendly, and she couldn't help feeling a surge of excitement from simply being noticed—sought out, in fact. Marcus hadn't noticed her in so long.

Janet was unsure how to answer Russ's question because she did not want her admission of spending so much time alone to seem like an invitation for his company, yet saying anything else would be a lie. She *did* spend most weekends at home alone, but he didn't need to know that her loneliness had left her feeling discarded and dismally unwanted.

Janet decided to change the subject to something safer than her solitude and ignored his question. *How's your mom?* she typed instead.

*She's good. I haven't been back since we had lunch. U probly no how she's doin better than I do since ur there every day,* he wrote, noticing her topic change and deciding that meant "yes" to his previous question.

*Not actually,* she typed in response, a little bothered that he had typed "no" instead of "know." She really hoped he knew the difference. *I work with long-term care patients, and your mom is only there short-term while she recovers. She'll be able to go home soon.*

They typed back and forth for a little while longer about his mom's condition then more small talk about the weather ensued.

*So what r u goin 2 do tmrw if the electricity goes out?* he asked.

*Stay in bed all day,* she answered immediately and clicked enter before becoming acutely aware of the possible implications he might read into her statement if his mind wandered in the wrong direction. When she and Marcus were younger and utterly in love, back when they couldn't get enough of each other, Marcus would have treated that statement as an enticement, and she would've spent her day doing more than snuggling under the covers.

Janet pictured how Marcus would have stuck out his chest like Superman and declared, "Challenge accepted," like the character Barney would do in an episode of his favorite television show *How I Met Your Mother.*

*Sounds like a plan,* Russ replied. *Well, make sure u charge ur cell phone in case we lose power so you can call me if you need anything. May get rough tmrw.*

He gave her his phone number, and she assured that she'd call if she needed anything. Having him offer to run to her assistance made Janet feel good about herself, but she had no intentions of calling. If she needed help, her parents were right across town, and she knew her worrisome mom would send her dad to help if she needed anything.

A little anxious from the whistling winds outside after they said goodnight and Russ signed off, Janet decided to sleep on the couch with the television on in case she woke up and wanted a quick update of the storm situation. Russ's cautioning comments had left her slightly concerned.

Surprisingly, despite the loudening rain and tree limbs grazing the roof, Janet slept soundly curled up on the sofa and wrapped in a thick quilt with Mr. Happy lying at her feet, her toes tucked under his belly.

When she woke to the beeping television at six o'clock Saturday morning, Janet's internal clock thought it was midnight from the darkness outside. A flashing blue line scrolled across the bottom of the screen listing the counties under the current watches and warnings. Hers was included, which was no surprise. The newscasters kept going on and on, but Janet didn't panic because that's what they did—make a big deal out of everything, which is why she never trusted the news, people who took the tiniest stories and blew the details completely out of proportion.

Although from the noise going on outside, maybe they were being truthful and not exaggerating this time. Overnight, Hurricane Shelby had apparently shifted unlike they'd expected and looked to hit her town much harder than anticipated. Usually her town just got a lot of rain from these things, and by the time a hurricane reached them, it would be downgraded to a tropical storm. Shelby wasn't following the usual pattern though, and seemed to be picking up steam rather than losing momentum as it struck the nearby coast.

She stretched her arms to the ceiling and yawned before sleepily standing up and walking into the shadowy kitchen to make a pot of coffee. She flicked on the light over the stove, so she could see to fill the pitcher with water and scoop medium roast grounds into the filter.

From the kitchen, she heard the regular programming interrupted by meteorologists giving weather updates and offering tips to residents in the storm's projected path. As she lay around lazily watching movies all day, Janet kept an eye on the bottom right corner of the screen where a map highlighted the eastern counties under various watches and warnings, and Janet had watched her county go from yellow to red in the last half hour.

The weather had been rather rough all day long. She had somewhat expected that when she went to sleep the night before from the increasingly cooler temperatures and news reports of the past week tracking the tropical storm through the Gulf, but she hadn't expected Saturday morning's reports of the storm upgrading to hurricane strength overnight or for the worst part of the storm to hit her town head-on.

Janet's town lay close enough to the coast that they'd usually get one rough storm each year, but it laid far enough inland that the storms usually weren't too terrible, bringing only heavy rain and wind without disastrous flooding or destruction.

This one, however, appeared to be mounting as the storm of the century for her town according to the meteorologists on her local television network. The eye had turned over the last few hours and was embarking on land with the path destined just west of her town, meaning they would be hit with the hardest winds, and inches of rain would be dumped on the city in a short amount of time, causing worries of flood on the low-lying streets.

Above the noise of the television and Mr. Happy's worried whines, the howls of the wind started to gain momentum, amplifying the hammering of raindrops on the front windows. Bad weather had always frightened Janet, and bad weather plus being alone just didn't mix. Mr. Happy seemed more unnerved than she, his whole body trembled beneath her hand as she rubbed him soothingly while they sat cuddled on the sofa.

"It's okay, boy. I'm scared, too," she assured him, dreading waiting out this storm at the house by herself and slightly tempted to call Russ like he'd suggested the night before during their chat, but deciding that was a bad idea.

The cell phone lying on the floor beside the couch rang, cutting through the noise of the storm outside. Janet quickly ambled back into the living room to pick it up. Caller ID said Julia was on the other end of the line.

"Hey," Janet answered. "I guess you're calling to cancel the movie date, huh?"

"Yep, how'd you guess?" Julia rhetorically joked, the reason for not taking Lucy to the movie theater being quite obvious. Janet sat down on the couch and muted the television to better hear her sister.

"It looks really bad outside. We decided last night to go over to Mom and Dad's today, but the rain was already too rough this morning, so we stayed at home. Zack didn't want to risk being on the roads, but I'd much rather be at their house than here, wouldn't you?" Julia asked her older sister.

Going to her parents' house to ride out the storm hadn't even occurred to Janet, who was used to doing everything on her own. Julia, however, still turned to Mom and Dad for everything, just like she always had growing up. Julia had let her mom tie her shoelaces until she was in second grade whereas Janet had insisted on tying her own starting in four-year-old kindergarten.

A booming crack outside startled Janet, and for a brief second the house went dark before the lights flickered back on, making her wish she'd had the foresight to pack up and go to her parents' house rather than being all alone.

"I think I'll be all right here by myself. I hope they have supplies at their house," Janet wondered out loud of her parents.

"Are you kidding me?" Julia sounded astonished. "You know Mom keeps those kinds of things on hand all the time, always prepared for anything."

Thinking of the first aid kit and case of bottled water that sat on a shelf above Sandra's washer and dryer, Janet agreed. "That's true. She probably has everything she'd need to save the world all tucked away in her purse!"

"Probably so! You know she was with me when I had to get my car tags renewed at the court house last month, and the security guard made her empty her purse because she had an aerosol can of hair spray, a sewing kit complete with scissors and needles, a cigarette lighter, and wire cutters in there. Wire cutters! What in the world she was carrying those for, I haven't a clue!" Julia laughed. "She said they were for her flowers or something."

As the satellite television searched to regain a signal, Janet stood up and walked into the kitchen to retrieve the batteries and candles from the shopping bags she'd set on the counter the afternoon before while holding the phone between her ear and shoulder so both hands could be free to go through her supplies. The preparations she'd taken by going to the department store before the storm were futile if the supplies remained in the bag, so she started unpacking the bags to be ready in the event the lights went out, which she felt would likely happen before the day ended from the looks of things outside.

She remembered back in college, she would be the one huddled up in the hallway with pillows, a blanket, and a flashlight while her roommates acted like nothing was wrong when a storm hit. One clap of thunder and Janet would be shaking while they made fun of her. She had always rather be safe than sorry.

"Hang on, Lucy wants to talk to her Aunt Janet," Julia said. Janet could hear the mother and daughter talking in the background, whispering "say hello" on the other end of the line as Julia handed the little girl the phone.

"Hello," the little voice answered.

"Hi, pretty girl! Sorry we're going to miss the movie! We'll go again soon, okay?" Janet encouraged, hoping her niece wasn't too disappointed.

"Okay," Lucy replied. "Momma says we're gonna pway camping!" she exclaimed excitedly.

"She did, huh? Well that sounds like fun!" Janet said. "Are you going to build a tent?"

"Yep, I am! Momma says we're gonna have fwashwights and peanut butter samwiches and tell stories!" The little girl's slight lisp became more pronounced when she got excited and started talking fast.

"All right, then! You're going to have a blast! Just make sure you take an umbrella so you don't get wet."

"We're not weally camping, Aunt Janet," Lucy solemnly assured her. "We're putting the tent inside. Do you want to come pway camping with us?" the little girl implored.

"I'm sorry, baby. The weather's really bad so I can't drive over there now. I'm sorry," Janet apologized.

"That's okay," she said disappointedly. "Here's my momma."

Janet sat candles on the kitchen counter next to the refrigerator and got a manual can opener from the drawer to place with the cans of ravioli next to the microwave. Furrowing her brow, she wondered how she'd heat the ravioli were the electricity to go out and wished she'd thought of that sooner. At least, like Lucy on her camping extravaganza, Janet could have peanut butter and bread, and the jelly in the door of the fridge should stay cool enough for a while.

"Well, Janet, I guess I better go. Don't wanna waste all my cell phone battery in case electricity goes out soon," Julia explained. "Stay safe! Talk to you later!"

Janet said goodbye to her sister and, as she emptied the ice from the icemaker into a small cooler, speculated whether or not she should catch some water in a bathtub then decided it couldn't hurt to be over prepared. Her mom had probably already caught every bathtub and sink full of water, possibly even brought in five gallon buckets to fill up. Janet wished she had that protective instinct; it would really come in handy in times like these.

A glimpse of the ominous sky outside through the window by her bed gave Janet chills as she passed through her master bedroom to run water in the bathtub. She took the rest of the bags of candles with her, setting one down on each surface she passed. As long as she carried a lighter in her pocket, she'd be able to find a candle in a hurry if the house went dark again.

With the tub filled, Janet carried the shopping bags to her closet to pack away what she hadn't used. She shook her head as she pulled a shoebox from one of the bags, silently scolding herself for her rash purchase the day before.

She had hurried into the store after work to grab the necessities for storm preparation, but she'd pushed her buggy down the aisle past a clearance rack and couldn't resist stopping for a moment to check the prices.

An innocent moment of price-gazing turned into a thirty-minute meeting of shopaholics anonymous, checking the sizes and prices of every shoe in the whole sale section then browsing through the adjoining shelves of scarves and hats that had just been put on display in the past week anticipating the cooler weather brought on by the cold front accompanying the storm system.

Unable to resist a good bargain, Janet tucked a discounted pair of walnut brown, peep-toe stilettos in her cart alongside a box of double A batteries. Then, as she started to push the cart away, she quickly snatched a ruffled scarf, dyed the same dark hue as her shoes, off the rack before quickly walking straight to the checkout counter, not giving herself time to think twice about the impulse purchases.

Standing in the closet, Janet opened the shoebox and decided to try on the shoes before putting them on her hanging shoe rack. She kicked off her slippers and balanced on her left foot to pull her pajama pants up over her knee and slip on the first stiletto and then switched on the other foot, holding onto the doorframe with one hand to keep herself steady.

As though on a runway, she sexily put one foot in front of the other and strutted across the bedroom until the toe of her shoe caught the hem of her pajamas, and Janet stumbled toward the bed, thankful for a soft mattress to catch her fall.

"Oomph," she grunted, bracing her weight on her hands and pushing herself upright. She slipped both shoes off then shimmied out of the pajama pants, stepping out of the legs and leaving them lying on the floor. She walked back into the closet and rifled through her cocktail dresses, looking for the coral pencil dress that had been hanging unworn in the back of her closet and with the tags still on it.

She pulled her worn t-shirt over her head and tossed it to the floor then stepped into the dress, guided it over her hips, slipped her arms through the cap sleeves, and zipped it up on the side, a little surprised that it still fit just right, perhaps even better than it had when she'd bought it.

For over a year, the only clothes she'd bought had been picked out with the anticipation of getting really fat, so most of them had high waists and spandex.

Not this dress.

The linen clung to every curve of her figure so well that the first glimpse of herself in the mirror had actually brought a tear to her eye when she'd tried it on. She'd bought the dress and hung it in her closet, never even showing it to Marcus.

She slipped the heels back on her feet and wrapped the matching scarf around her neck, tying it loosely in the front then stepped back to look at herself in the mirror.

*This should get even Marcus's attention*, she thought and smiled knowing there was one man whose attention it would definitely claim, even if it didn't attract her husband.

The ringing cell phone interrupted her fashion show. Janet looked and was surprised by the number she saw on the screen.

"Hello?" she answered.

"Janet, hi. This is Susan. Can you come in?" the nursing home human resources director asked.

"Now?" Janet said, smoothing her hands over the fabric, turning one way and then another to see herself from all angles in the glass.

"Yes," was the reply from the other end of the line. "I'm sorry to bother you like this when you're probably getting your own house ready for the storm, but we're calling in all staff members to help secure the patients before it gets worse here. How soon can you be here?"

Janet looked at Mr. Happy and then at her own reflection in the mirror, knowing she didn't want to face this bad weather alone. Riding out the storm surrounded by people, even at work, seemed a much better option. She disliked leaving Mr. Happy alone and worried he might get scared and tear up something in the house, but she had no other choice. Knowing she'd already fed and watered him earlier that day, he should be fine until the storm was over and she could come back home.

"I can be there in about fifteen minutes, weather permitting," she answered. "Do I have time to change?"

"We need everyone here as soon as possible. If you take time to change, the weather will just get worse. The sooner you can leave home, the safer it'll be for you to drive. Can't you just change when you get here?" the nurse fretfully replied.

"Yeah, I didn't think about that," Janet stated. "I'll see you in a few."

She hung up the phone and bent over to pat the pup on his head.

"I'm sorry buddy," she apologized, the sad look in Mr. Happy's eyes crushing her with guilt as she grabbed a pair of pink scrubs from the closet and quickly tossed them in a tote bag.

Janet hurried into the kitchen and tossed the tote bag over her shoulder. The wind outside sounded fierce, as she picked up her purse from the kitchen counter and started to sort through it for her keys. After taking her keys out of the pocket on her purse and pulling the hood of her raincoat over her head, Janet wished she hadn't left her umbrella in the car the afternoon before. Although with the way the wind was blowing, an umbrella probably wouldn't matter much.

Chapter 17

She ran to the car with her bag of clothes and purse both hanging on her left arm, holding her keys ready in her right hand, stilettos tromping through the puddles and rainwater splattering up drenching the dry-clean only fabric on the bottom hem of her dress.

"Great," she muttered as she slammed the door, wishing she'd thought twice about wearing that dress out of the house. Not only did the pencil design limit her maneuverability, but it seemed like such a shame to waste its first outing on an ugly night like this.

Water beaded on the raincoat and poured all over the seat of her car. Janet hated driving in the rain. She longed for the sunshine she'd scoffed at a week ago. With the key in the ignition, she backed out of the driveway and turned to pull out on the road.

The images the television crews had shown in the last hour of the coast several hours south of Janet's town flashed into her mind as she began the drive to the nursing home. Since those images had been taken, the storm had stalled over the water and gained even more strength, its threat becoming more and more violent. The meteorologists and reporters on scene showed the floodwaters, the swells, the homes, the towns that had already been destroyed over the last twenty-four hours. Photos of people who were trying to evacuate too late being rescued from drowning cars worried Janet as she drove through the puddles of standing water.

As far as she knew, no one had ever been forced to evacuate her town. They were far enough away from the coastline and above sea level, so flooding had never been much of an issue, but the sheer strength of the storm itself was Janet's fear.

She thought about Jesus' disciples out on the boat in the middle of the sea as the storm approached. The seas were raging. That was how she felt right now. She felt she was out in the middle of this ocean of life on a dinky little boat. Any minute now, the waves were going to topple it over, and she was going to sink. She'd seen the storm coming, but she couldn't get out of the way, and there was nothing she could do.

She remembered how, in the story as the disciples feared, they looked out at the water and saw Jesus walking toward them, how Peter got out of the boat and walked on the water to Jesus, and how he didn't sink until he took his eyes off his Lord.

She was afraid to get out of the boat. She was afraid to be like Peter. Janet didn't think she could walk on water. In times of doubt, she really wasn't sure she even believed the story. She believed the Bible, but walking on water was a miracle, and Janet wasn't sure she believed in miracles anymore. They made for great stories, but that wasn't real life.

In real life, Peter would've just sunk. In real life, the storm would've tossed the ship around. It would have destroyed the masts, it would have destroyed the navigation systems. If the boat itself didn't get turned over, they'd still be stranded in the middle of the sea, just hoping someone would come along and help.

As she turned at the stop sign, the highway was, thankfully, nearly deserted. She guessed everyone else had the better idea of staying at home. She was only a few miles away from work, where she'd change out of these wet clothes into her scrubs. She drove, thinking of all this rain and how just days ago Marcus had said he'd love to see a raindrop, that he'd almost forgotten what rain looked like after the dry season in Iraq.

She was driving in enough rain right now for both of them. She wished he were there. If he were there, she'd never be out driving in this rain. She'd be at home with him, candles ready in case the lights went out, probably reading a book, not wanting to get too engrossed in a television show or movie just for the lights to go out in the middle of it.

As she turned in the parking lot, the wind suddenly grew worse. Closing the door, she tried to run toward the front door of the building. The wind was blowing so hard that she had to be cautious of each step she took and wished that she'd taken the time to change out of her new heels, guessing they would likely be ruined after being submerged in inches of water.

The wind pressed against the heavy door to the building, making it difficult for Janet to open.

"Here," Russ said, hurrying up from behind her and ripping the door open, ushering her quickly inside.

"What are you doing here?" Janet asked, breathless as she unbuttoned her raincoat and started to shake it off before throwing it on the floor on top of the mound of wet umbrellas.

"You're welcome." He smiled despite her not bothering to thank him for opening the door and saving her from getting even more soaked standing out in the rain. He then shook the rain from his hair and wiped his face.

"Thanks," she mumbled, tousling her own hair to shake out some of the water while trying not to notice how his wet t-shirt outlined the muscles of his chest.

"My mom called, said she was scared, so I jumped in the car and rushed over," Russ explained to answer Janet's inquiry as he stepped back and looked her over from head to toe, making her face flush. He grinned devilishly, and her pulse quickened as she watched a raindrop trace the line of his square jaw. When her eyes met his, the appreciation for her skin-tight dress, which clung to her even more now that it was damp, showed deeply in his gaze.

"I don't know what you're doing so dressed up, but I like it," he said huskily, his desire evident as he unconsciously took a step toward her.

Janet smiled nervously then quickly excused herself to check on her patients, backing away for fear that he could see her heart beating through the tight dress. She turned and walked away as hastily as possible while trying not to swing her hips, knowing he was watching every move she made.

As she turned the corner from the foyer into the patients' hallway, Janet met chaos.

The inclement weather had disrupted many of the patients' routines and had them afraid and disoriented, either of which symptoms was difficult enough to handle on its own; combined, fear and confusion posed a grave dilemma.

One gray-haired woman sat sniveling quietly by the door to her room. Her neighbor in the next room ranted about needing his glasses, which sat squarely on his nose. Down the hall, a nurse checked the blood pressure of a man who complained of chest pains while another nurse coaxed multiple patients down the hall toward the common areas.

Patients who could walk around under their own power or with the aid of a walker were strolling up and down the halls like they did every day, only with a frantic haste toward the cafeteria, some stopping to check on their neighbors, others hassling the nurses to find out what was going on, some following aimlessly and oblivious to anything around them.

All the while, thunder boomed and rain crashed down on the building, heightening the noise level throughout the facility.

Janet hurried to the nurses' lounge where she could change into the scrubs she'd grabbed as she ran out of the house. She changed into the bubble gum pink top and pants and carefully folded the coral dress and set it on the top shelf of her locker while feeling selfishly a little disappointed that she wouldn't get to see the passionate look in Russ's eyes again like he had looked at her in that dress.

She muttered an obscenity under her breath as she emptied the tote bag out onto the floor in search of her second clog, which was, inconveniently, still lying on the floor of her closet at home. *Maybe no one will notice,* she thought, resigning to looking like an idiot all night in scrubs and stilettos, hoping her ankles and calves could hold out, but knowing blisters awaited in her future.

She hung her wet raincoat on the hook on the back of the bathroom door and pulled her damp, wavy hair up, twisting it into a loose bun on top of her head, a few short pieces falling out and curling around her face.

The small twenty-inch television in the nurses' lounge was set to the weather channel, which was running the story of the reporter who had been forced to retreat indoors because the wind had suddenly gotten so violent on scene in the next town over. The rain-drenched woman in the poncho was saying it was headed right toward Janet's town.

As she strode down the hallway, the loud *swish-click* of her squishy-wet heels on the linoleum was drowned out by the ruckus of the busy staff trying to maintain order.

She could feel it coming, her palms sweating with nervous energy. The menacing storm was headed right for them, and, knowing the next few hours were going to be arduous, all she could do was brace for impact.

"Janet, good to have you here," her frenzied director said, patting Janet on the shoulder and talking as they walked toward the central nurse's station. "This is what we need to do. All rooms with windows need to be evacuated. We want to move everyone as calmly as possible, so we're having all the patients taken to the cafeteria for dinner while we set up extra beds in the single private rooms along the interior corridors. They are now doubles.

"Alzheimer's ward needs to be closely monitored, especially if the electricity goes out. It'll take a few minutes for the backup generator to kick in, so we'll need everyone around to keep them calm." She paused to take a breath.

"Extra flashlights will be passed out to all capable patients just as a precaution once we move them back to the rooms. For now, I need you on bed duty. Roll 'em, twist 'em, turn 'em, I don't care what you have to do, but get as many beds set up in secure rooms as you possibly can," the director barked, pointing her finger at Janet as she hurried away.

Thirty minutes later, Janet took a five-second break to rest against the bed she was moving into one of the last rooms in that hallway. The hall was empty since all the patients were being held in the common areas, but she was running out of time because dinner would soon be over. She took advantage of the moment of silence to step out of the heels that pained her poor feet then sat down on the corner of the rolling bed to rub her soles.

"Cute shoes." Russ laughed, leaning against the wall where he'd just turned the corner.

"Thanks," she said haughtily, rolling her eyes.

He sauntered over to her, slowly, purposefully.

Kneeling at her feet, his strong hands took her right foot and began massaging circles into her sole with his thumbs.

"Oh," she moaned unconsciously, her eyelids closing heavily.

Russ rubbed her other foot for a minute or so until her knees became such jell-o that she was thankful for the firm bed beneath her. He stood slowly, his hand gently reaching around her waist and pulling her to her bare feet.

In an instant, the exhilaration of this man plummeted to the pit of Janet's stomach, and she pushed him away gently, her palm against his rigid chest.

"You can't do this," she whispered. "I love my husband."

"Your husband doesn't look at you the way I do, and you know it," he whispered back hoarsely.

Janet swallowed, keeping him at arms' length. He was right. Marcus hadn't looked at her longingly or lovingly in the past two years.

"But he's still my husband," she whimpered softly, feeling emotionally trapped by this man almost as much as she had felt trapped in a marriage to a man who had crushed her hopes and dreams. "That's all that..."

A crash interrupted her sentence and caused Janet to squeal. Russ hurriedly pushed her back onto the bed in the doorway and stood between her and the noise at the end of the deserted hallway. Something from outside had slammed against the metal exterior door, and it was starting to clang quietly against its frame.

"Sorry, I didn't mean to push you. Just reaction," Russ said as he reached out to help her back to her feet.

"That's okay," Janet mumbled as she pushed herself up, refusing the hand he offered.

"I need to get back to work," she asserted, staring him directly in the eyes. "Would you mind pushing this bed against the wall in that room?"

"Sure, glad to help," he answered jadedly, visibly giving up on getting a reciprocal response from Janet after being so obviously shot down again.

"Thanks, I'm going to go let the director know the patients can be brought back to this hall now," she explained as she put her shoes back on and started down the hallway, the lump in her throat growing with every step. Part of her wanted to revel in the blood rush Russ caused within her, and the look in his eyes was enough to make any woman weak, but if her husband didn't look at her or make her feel like that, then she'd just have to go the rest of her life reconciled to never feel that way again.

She'd made a vow to love only him for better or worse. Their relationship definitely fell into the "worse" category these days, but that was the cross she had to bear, even if it meant never having children or grandchildren and never getting the future she had always dreamed of having. And she couldn't spend the rest of her life angry at Marcus for turning his back on her, or they would both be miserable.

Shaking her head for comparing her marriage to a cross, Janet joined the crowd in the cafeteria and began the process of moving patients back to their rooms as dinner ended.

Getting the patients settled for bed wasn't as hard as the nurses had anticipated. While some patients objected to moving beds and sharing rooms, the short-term memory of many of the patients was so absent that they didn't even notice the changes.

Mrs. Tanner seemed to be the most upset of Janet's patients, but, fortunately, her husband was there to help Janet calm her down.

"But I can't see my roses! Why are you taking away my roses?" Lucille angrily demanded as Mr. Tanner and Janet tried to move her into a room Janet had prepared across the hall. She'd lain in the hospital bed crying until she'd fallen asleep with her husband soothingly stroking her hand, promising she'd see the roses when she woke up.

Janet pitied the poor man who sat in a chair by the bed, even though Janet had prepared him a cot. He didn't want to leave Lucille's side with her in such a confused state of mind. His expression as he stared at his wife's sobbing form was one of pure devotion, something Janet admired tremendously as she stepped out the room to settle her other patients.

Two hours later, Janet stood at the nurse's station and leaned over the counter with the other ladies watching the weather report on the desktop computer monitor. The loud rain rolling on the roof confirmed their account of the storm's progress, and the strain of the evening showed on the tired faces of the women at the counter.

"I wonder how bad it is outside," a young brunette mused nervously.

"I don't know, honey," one older, plump woman answered. The pictures they viewed online showed cars overturned and roofs partially blown off by the Category 3 winds at a small town that was closer to the coastline.

"We're safe here though. Nothing to be scared of," she assured. "Just listen to the wind outside. Our God made the wind and rain just as he made the sun to shine. He is in control, and that's enough for me."

Janet thought about the woman's words of wisdom: "He's in control, and that's enough for me." Janet wondered, *Is that enough for me?* thinking of Marcus and how many years of her life had been focused on him as her number one priority, and how the last couple of years had been focused on what she couldn't have out of life. Janet could hardly remember when her life centered around the one who really mattered, the one who was in control.

"Why don't we say a prayer for God to watch over us and everyone here through the storm? Is that okay?" the woman asked the younger nurses, who all nodded in response and bowed their heads.

Janet closed her eyes tightly as the other woman prayed. "Dear Lord, we come to you now to thank you for your many blessings. We especially thank you in advance for the protection you cast over us, our patients, our friends, and our families tonight. Your word says we must ask and believe you will answer our request, so I ask you now to keep us safe. We know that you are always in control and watching over us to help us through every situation. Show us how best to handle whatever challenges this storm may bring, and help us do what needs to be done to help those under our care. In your son, Jesus' name, Amen."

When she opened her eyes, they glistened with tears. Janet wanted to ask God to help her let go of her dream of having a happy family, but she couldn't. She still wanted that dream to come true.

The hours ahead were rough. Janet had never seen a storm this bad in all her life. The winds were blowing so hard and debris outside was being tossed around. She could hear debris hitting cars and breaking windows. She was terrified. They all were. The nurses had moved all the patients to interior rooms away from all the windows, which turned out to be a very difficult task.

Taking an Alzheimer's patient and disrupting his or her routine were always trying. Alzheimer's patients needed routine. They needed whatever sense of familiarity they could grasp. Taking that away by waking them up in the middle of the night had them so disoriented that it took everything the nurses could do just to calm them down. Some of them weren't able to be calmed and had to be separated from the other patients and given sedatives.

Janet hated seeing these people being medicated in such a way, but under the circumstances she didn't see any other options. They had to be kept calm, so they could be kept safe. The patients didn't understand that. So many of them didn't know where they were some days, anyway. You take away what little element they do understand, and it was just pure chaos.

Janet shook her head. She was exhausted. The other nurses were exhausted, but there wasn't any time for rest. There wasn't time to be scared. There wasn't time to worry about your vehicle sitting in the parking lot or worry about your family members because too much had to be done. Some of the patients had actually gotten injured in the move. One woman had fallen. Fortunately she appeared to have only been bruised. One patient with heart problems had had a spell, and the nurses knew there was no way an ambulance could get to them right now, so they were frantically trying to keep his heart rate down, to keep him calm, to assure him that everything would be okay.

Some patients were worried about their children and wanted to know where their kids were. They talked about their kids' bicycles being outside in the rain and how the bicycles were going to rust. Janet got so frustrated that she wanted to just scream out, "Your kid is thirty years old! His bicycle isn't in the parking lot! It's not going to rust! Just chill out!"

But of course her polite response was simply, "I'll check on it for you. The bicycle is going to be fine."

With the patients all in bed, the nurses were able to take turns making rounds throughout the night since so many of them had come in to work through the storm. When Janet finished her rounds and settled on a cot in the common room to try to catch a quick nap before her turn was up again, she couldn't sleep with the noise from the storm outside. She checked her cell phone. No bars.

*Cell towers must be down*, she thought. Janet had wanted to call her parents to make sure they were okay, so not being able to get a signal was a little frustrating. Her phone was almost dead since she hadn't charged it in over twenty-four hours, and she hadn't thought to grab her charger before she left home.

She wondered if Marcus even knew what was going on. She just had a really rough night, and he probably wasn't even aware there had been a storm. *So much for having a help mate*, she thought to herself.

Janet just wanted to sleep. Her feet hurt because of those stupid stilettos. Oh, how she hated those ugly clogs she wore every day to work, but she wished she had them right now. The rain was still pouring, but the wind had died down over the last hour or so, and it would soon be morning, time to start assessing the damage.

The administration had decided to wait until lunch to move the patients again. It had taken so long to get them settled, no one wanted to disturb them again as soon as they woke up.

The facility had lost electricity at one point during the night but only for a few minutes. Janet didn't know what they would have done without the backup generators. As it were, the overhead lights in the patients' rooms were turned off, anyway, while they slept, so most of them never knew the electrical system had blown. Janet walked over to the loveseat and sorted through the magazines on the coffee table by the light of the lamp on the side table. Being not interested in Diabetic cooking or *Senior Living* magazines, Janet picked up a Sunday School booklet left by one of the local churches and began turning the pages. Her own Bible at home was shamefully dusty from being untouched so long, and Janet hadn't attended Sunday School in several months now.

The first lesson she read began with a scripture from Daniel 9. She read starting with verse 17, "Now therefore, O our God, hear the prayer of thy servant, and his supplications, and cause thy face to shine upon thy sanctuary that is desolate, for the Lord's sake. O my God, incline thine ear, and hear; open thine eyes, and behold our desolations, and the city which is called by thy name: for we do not present our supplications before thee for our righteousnesses, but for thy great mercies. O Lord, hear; O Lord, forgive; O Lord, hearken and do; defer not, for thine own sake, O my God: for thy city and thy people are called by thy name."

"Lord, listen. Lord, forgive. Lord, hear and act," she repeated softly. Maybe all she really needed was to simply ask God to show mercy and make her feel whole again. *Can it really be that easy?* she thought to herself.

Janet had clung to her faith through the trying months of fertility treatments, but her motives for having a child were selfish and never focused on what God's will was for her life. She'd wanted to be a mother. She'd wanted to have the family her friends had.

Perhaps, she wondered, she had needed to experience real disappointment to realize how out of focus her life was. Even when she had thought she was living as a good Christian, Janet's life revolved around what she wanted and needed from God rather than what God wanted and needed from her.

"True joy comes only from the Lord," her mom had always taught, but Janet had never fully invested her hopes in the Lord, relying more on herself and her circumstances for happiness rather than the joy from within. She couldn't blame Marcus for the loss of her joy, which should have been anchored on the Lord, not man.

# Chapter 18

Marcus sat in front of the computer screen with his webcam on, Skype open. He'd been trying to send her messages and call for hours now, but no one answered. His calls wouldn't go through. He didn't know where she was. He hadn't talked to her in days. He didn't know if she was at home.

He'd just gotten back to base that afternoon from his latest mission and heard about the storm on the East Coast. He'd been worried about her and been trying to call ever since.

He'd called his parents, and they were fine, but they said they hadn't heard from her.

He'd called her parents, who also said they hadn't heard from her and were starting to get worried because their calls weren't going through either.

Her mom said she wasn't scheduled to work tonight, and they'd thought about driving over to her house to check on her, but the weather was just too bad. They'd boarded up their windows and brought the pets inside and had plenty of water in case the electricity had gone out.

Marcus wondered if she'd thought to stock up on those things, if she had bottled water, if she had food in case she was without electricity for several days. His heart quivered imagining Janet trapped at home, cuddled in the corner of the closet with pillows and her cell phone, twitching involuntarily each time the thunder boomed overhead, terrified.

He was usually the one to prepare for situations like storms. His survival training made him more aware of the necessity of preparations than she would ever be. She had no survival skills other than knowing where the scented candles were if the lights went out. He disliked the smell of candles, so she didn't burn them often. Sometimes, he half-wondered if she wanted the electricity to go out for just a little while so she'd have an excuse to burn them.

Right now, Marcus just wanted to know where she was and whether or not she was all right. It dawned on him that maybe this is how she felt, wondering where he was every day. This was how she'd felt for the past nine months, sitting at home waiting for a phone call, waiting to hear that he was okay.

In that moment of epiphany, he was starting to understand why she had been so distant and borderline depressed. Nervously pacing his room, Marcus decided that he couldn't go about his daily routine as a soldier worrying whether or not she was safe from this storm.

*How does she do it, how does she go about her routine every day worrying about me?* Marcus pondered, shaking his head dispiritedly. *This is no way to live, just waiting,* he thought.

A Bible verse popped into his head at that last thought: "But they that wait up on the Lord shall renew their strength; they shall mount up with wings as eagles; they shall run, and not be weary; they shall walk, and not faint," Marcus quoted to himself.

He had been waiting on the Lord. And he was waiting now, but he was worried. He was scared. He could only imagine being scared and worried like this every day for months, and sorrow overwhelmed him for putting her through this and for being so unsympathetic to how she felt.

"Lord, I'm sorry I haven't been the husband she needed," Marcus pleaded, dropping to sit on his twin bed and folding his hands prayerfully in his lap. "Please let her be all right, and I'll do my best to make it up to her, to show her how much I love her, to give her everything I can, everything I promised her in the beginning."

He didn't blame her anymore for being detached, for locking her heart away so it wouldn't ache all the time. He hadn't known what the torture felt like to live waiting for phone calls.

Until now.

Looking over the debris-littered garden, the devastation began to sink in for Janet. The crepe myrtle trees lay on the ground; tiny lavender blooms scattered and stuck to every solid surface. The tables and chairs on the terrace had been chained down, but they had all blown over, and one of the tables had broken as it hit the ground. Janet stood on the brick terrace under the leaning awning and surveyed the garden that had been so beautiful only a few days before as she'd sat outside eating lunch.

In the center of the courtyard, standing just as pretty as ever and seemingly untouched by the storm, was one yellow rose bush with blooms still intact. Janet remembered Mrs. Tanner looking at the roses every morning, and something the old woman had said suddenly stood out in Janet's mind: "When I look at these roses, I know I'm not alone."

Mr. Tanner came to stand beside Janet. He'd been at the nursing home when Janet had arrived the afternoon before and had stayed by Lucille's side all night long.

*If only more husbands were like him,* Janet thought as she greeted the old man.

"Looks bleak, doesn't it, dear?" he commented, not really expecting a response. "But everything turned out okay, and I bet this garden will be prettier than it's ever been next spring!"

Janet nodded, trying to release a bit of the strain from the last twenty-four hours.

"How do you do it?" she asked.

"How do I do what, dear?"

"How do you stay so positive all the time? Please don't take this the wrong way or let it upset you. Mrs. Lucille's a wonderful woman, but how do you maintain a relationship when she doesn't even know who you are sometimes?" she questioned.

"It's easy." He took a deep breath thinking of how to explain his feelings to the young woman then cleared his throat. "The Lord gives each person a certain amount of time, and each person's time and experiences will be different. We don't know how long we have. We don't know how long *they* have. We'll have good times, and we'll have bad times, but it's all a wonderful blessing.

"He blessed me with fifty-seven years with Lucille. We built a house, raised four beautiful children, we have seven grandchildren, two great-grandchildren, and I wouldn't have any of that without her. Even in her sickness, she's still the same woman, and I owe my life to her," he continued.

"I know you love her, but how do you cope with what has happened to her and how it's affected your life?"

"Well, obviously, this isn't the future I had planned for us. It's not the retirement I'd pictured, but this is what the Lord has given me and he knows best and he is faithful. When she first became sick, I was scared. She didn't know enough about what was going on to be scared, but I did. I knew that as she slipped away, I would have to watch the woman I love forget me."

Mr. Tanner turned to face Janet. "And I had a choice to make. I could try to do it all myself, to keep her at home, or I could bring her here for someone else to take care of. And that was the hardest decision I've ever had to make," he said shaking his head. "God doesn't say that our lives are going to be easy, that every decision is going to be clear-cut and simple. I wanted desperately for her to be able to stay at home. I felt like I owed it to her, to be able to take care of her like that. I didn't want to bring her to the nursing home."

He smiled and shrugged his shoulders. "And one day the Lord just told me that I couldn't do it by myself. And, no, I wasn't going to have the retirement I'd always dreamed of, and yes, Lucille was only going to get worse, but she didn't know what was happening and that the right thing for me to do would be to give her the best care possible, which meant leaving it up to the professionals, letting people like you give her what she needed."

"I bet that was hard for you, bringing her here," Janet said. "But you're so faithful to come visit her! She's very lucky."

"It hasn't been so bad. I am able to come here and spend time with her every day and still be able to do the things that God wants me to do. It took me a little while to realize that I'm not the one who is sick. See, I'm old, but as long as I'm alive, God has a plan for me. As long as I'm still kickin', he has something he wants me to do."

The old man's point dug home to Janet as she realized that she'd been so frustrated with God not jumping onboard with her plan that she hadn't considered that his plan might be different.

"So you want to know how I stay positive?" Mr. Tanner asked.

"Yes, sir, I do."

"Well, I stay on *his* path and I trust *him* that everything that happens in my life is something he has allowed to come to pass and that he will give me the strength and the wisdom to not just get through it but to overcome it, and to be a better witness for him because of it." He paused. "And seeing Lucille happy, you know, even though she's lost most of her memories, she's still happy—that's worth it all."

The lump in Janet's throat grew and grew. She could scarcely contain her sobs. She mustered what little strength she had to conceal her sobs, the teardrops slowly trickled out of the corners of her eyes and down her cheeks. She stood resolutely, shoulders slightly shaking as she took in all the old man had said.

He was in the middle of his crisis. The woman he loved was slipping further and further away, and he could do nothing to help her condition. Yet he was still positive despite knowing that things were only going to get worse.

For Janet, the man she loved would soon be coming home, and if she put her trust in the Lord as this man had done, she realized that things would only get better.

"Are you okay?" he asked her.

"I think so," Janet nodded. "What you said about God having a plan just made me think about my own life. This is not what I had planned for myself. There are so many things I wanted out of my life that I can't have, and I don't know how to accept that. I don't know how to stay positive. I guess I have to find a way to let go of those dreams and find new ones."

Mr. Tanner patted Janet on her shoulder as he faced her and talked to her like a loving grandfather would. "Dear, the future rarely turns out anything like what we expect or want. You have to accept that. And every time you start to think about what you've lost or what you say you can't have, every time that comes into your mind, you tell yourself that God is in control and that he loves you and that he is going to bless you. That's it!" he said, making it sound so simple.

Janet half-smiled as she stared out at the yellow rose bush. "That's it, huh? Then what?"

"Then you thank him for what he has given you, and you praise him for what he has promised to give you because you can praise the hurt away. You just have to trust him," he finished.

Janet knew in that moment that the roses were her rainbow, proof of God's promise that she had never been nor would ever be alone. She'd never face a day without God to help her through whatever it may bring.

She said goodbye to Mr. Tanner and thanked him for their talk then Janet went back inside to get back to work. She thought when she got married that she and Marcus would be spending their lives together, helping each other through the difficult times. She'd since learned that she couldn't depend on another person to satisfy her longings because people are human—they will disappoint. But God will never disappoint if one's wishes are based on his divine will rather than on personal desires.

Smiling all morning despite her tired, aching feet, Janet and her coworkers proficiently facilitated a semblance of normalcy for their patients despite the interruption of the daily routine by moving rooms again. The east side of the building had suffered a few broken windows, but a clean-up crew had already started clearing away the glass and planned to have the rooms ready in a day or two. Patients on all of the other wings were able to be move back to their private rooms by noon on Sunday, and the director released the extra nurses as replacements arrived, which took a while because of downed trees along highways and damages on local neighborhoods.

Considering she'd be going home to an empty house, Janet offered to stay so other nurses could go home to their families sooner.

By mid-afternoon, she took her first break of the day, getting a turkey sandwich from the cafeteria and sitting down in the lounge sofa to enjoy a few minutes of resting her feet as she kicked off the stilettos and propped her bare soles on the coffee table. The local cable channel happened to be showing pictures sent in by the general public. Janet recognized a nearby street with fallen power lines, which is probably why they were still running on generator power.

The destruction in the photos was worse than Janet had ever seen in her town, but so far no deaths or serious injuries had been reported, the newscaster informed, which was what mattered most.

She chewed a bite of the sandwich quickly, thankful to be eating something that didn't come out of a vending machine considering she'd been making do on peanut butter crackers and candy bars for the last twenty hours.

"The worst damage reported thus far is located in an older neighborhood, where residents are describing what may have been a tornado that spun up sometime during the evening several hours before the heart of the storm reached the town. Many century-old trees fell onto nearby houses, causing a lot of damage. Emergency crews are working behind me to clear away enough debris to be able to go in and..."

The rest of the reporter's sentence faded into the background of Janet's mind as her heart began pounding at the sight of her street on the screen.

She jumped to her feet, hopping around to put on her shoes in a hurry, grabbed her purse from the locker and hurried into the hall where she rushed to the nurse's station to find her boss.

"Linda, I've gotta go. I just saw on the news that my street was hit by a tornado last night," she frantically blurted. "I've gotta go home."

She rushed down the hallway toward the exit without waiting for the okay from her boss.

Her cell phone was completely dead, so she couldn't call her parents even if she were able to get service. Janet drove as quickly as possible toward her house but was slowed down by cleanup crews and debris in the streets and the drizzling rain.

"Oh, Lord, please help me get home quickly," she pleaded, terrified of what she would find when she arrived.

As she turned on the road that led to the entrance of her neighborhood, the destruction was devastating. The top branches of the towering oaks at the corner of the street on both sides had been broken and landed haphazardly across the road and lawns, crushing a car in one driveway and the mailbox across the street.

Janet started crying as she parked on the side of the road and got out to try to walk to her house since she obviously wouldn't make it by car.

Carefully watching every step she took, Janet tiptoed around broken shingles, cardboard bits, and limbs along the side of the road.

The trek to her house was long, especially for someone who'd been in high heels since yesterday afternoon without a good night's sleep. Although, had she been at home when this tornado touched down, Janet realized she would've gotten even less rest.

"Mr. Happy, please be at home," she cried to herself, stepping over a branch. A twinge in her ribcage scared her as she envisioned the hound hiding under her bed when the storm hit, and she could only hope he was safe.

She cut through a yard at the street corner to get to her house a little quicker, picking up the pace as much as her heels sticking into the wet ground would allow. Seeing her own backyard ahead, Janet tried to run, tears beginning to stream down her face.

The oak tree Marcus had carved their initials into still stood, but the majestic sight it used to be was no more. A couple of the larger branches had snapped and fallen under the weight of the wind, crushing through the roof on the far end of the house, crashing through the walls and exposing the interior of the guest bedroom to the outside.

Her heart sank, and she wasn't sure what to do. Janet was a little afraid of going inside with the tree laying on the roof like that. The sliding glass door on her back porch was broken, so she hurried around to the front of the house to try to get inside to assess the damage there.

"Houses can be fixed, houses can be fixed," she kept sobbing to herself as she saw that the front of her home looked okay other than the caving roof on the left side. One of the limbs was so massive that it had fallen all the way across the house into the front yard.

If any solace could be found in the disaster, Janet surprised herself by feeling a little relieved that the limbs had fallen on the end of the house with her spare bedrooms, away from the part of the house she used the most.

"Houses can be fixed," she repeated again and again, as she unlocked the front door, which was fortunately not under the fallen tree, and immediately began calling for Mr. Happy.

"Mr. Happy! Come here, boy! Mr. Happy!" she yelled as she tentatively stepped through the door frame onto soggy carpet.

Bounding from her bedroom, Mr. Happy ran as hard as his short legs could carry him, barreling into Janet as she bent down to meet him. She wrapped her arms around his little body and hugged him closely as they rocked gently back and forth, her tears falling on his head.

She tousled his floppy ears, "Are you okay, boy? I'm so sorry, I'm so sorry!" she begged for the pup's forgiveness, not wanting to let him go.

She knelt there on the floor for a brief moment, with her tear-stained cheek on his head and water soaking into the knees of her scrubs, before deciding she needed to think carefully and figure out what needed to be done next. The insurance company needed to be contacted, and she needed to inventory things that would need to be repaired and replaced.

But first things first, she had to find some different shoes.

Assuming it was safe to be in the house as long as she stayed away from the area hit by the trees, Janet went in the opposite direction toward her bedroom closet.

She picked up a pair of tennis shoes from the floor, her pair of backyard britches, and a t-shirt from the closet then walked over to her dresser to get a pair of socks. She quickly stripped out of her wet scrubs then pulled on the dry pair of jeans and top. Sitting on the corner of the bed and looking around her bedroom as she changed shoes, Janet would have never believed that the other end of her house was destroyed. Other than the rumpled comforter where Mr. Happy had obviously spent the night, the room looked untouched.

She stood up with a sigh and grabbed a suitcase from the top shelf of her closet and unzipped it on the bed. Janet began grabbing necessities—panties, bras, socks, jeans, a couple t-shirts, and shorts to sleep in—and she packed her cell phone charger first of all, extremely upset that she wasn't able to call her family for help.

She plundered quickly through her bathroom drawers to grab the basic toiletries and tossed them into her makeup bag then tucked it in the suitcase. Knowing she would have to carry everything all the way back to her car, Janet packed lightly, only bringing what she would need in the next forty-eight hours or so that could fit easily in her small rolling suitcase.

After retrieving her laptop from the living room and packing it away, Janet started to explore the house to see if there was anything she needed to do before driving over to her parents' house across town. Since power would obviously not be restored for a while, she went to the pantry to get an insulated tote and began to pack a few foods from the refrigerator, things she didn't want to spoil.

Hand on the handle of the freezer, Janet stopped herself and decided to leave it alone for now. Mostly everything would stay frozen for a day or so even without electricity, so she could deal with that after the roads were cleared and she had help.

Janet decided to go talk to her neighbors and see if anyone had a phone she could borrow, so she went back out through the front door, closing it securely behind her as soon as Mr. Happy had cleared the doorway.

Mrs. Suzanne stood in her front yard with her daughter-in-law while her son and grandsons piled up sticks and small limbs by the sidewalk. Her house was undamaged from what Janet could see, and she was grateful that is was her house rather than the old woman's. She and Marcus could bounce back a lot easier than a woman in her late sixties.

Walking over toward Mrs. Suzanne to see if someone in her family could lend her a phone, Janet heard a man's voice call her name from behind her.

Her dad walked speedily into her yard from the sidewalk, waving to get her attention, and then her mom scurried from behind him to embrace her daughter. Her dad's arms wrapped around both Janet and her mom, and he hugged both of the women tightly against his chest.

"It's okay, baby, it's okay," he soothed, stroking her hair as her shoulders shook with quiet sobs. "It can be rebuilt. You're okay."

"We saw it on the news and came right over. We've been trying to call you all day long!" Sandra exclaimed, obviously worried as she released her tight hold on her daughter and stepped back.

"I'm sorry," Janet sniffed and reached up to dry her eyes. "I got called into work yesterday afternoon and forgot to take my charger with me, so my phone has been dead *all day long*," she expressed her frustration, nodding slowly and dramatically when she said *all day long*.

"I was so worried that you were here when it happened!" Sandra choked. "Thank God you weren't home!"

"Have you talked to Marcus?" her dad asked.

"No, like I said, I haven't had a phone. I wonder if he even knows about the storm," she said. "He was out on a mission, so I haven't talked to him in a couple days."

"Here, let me get that suitcase, and we'll go back to our house so you can get a shower and…"—he paused mid-sentence— "we'll come back here later after the roads are cleared. Okay?"

"Okay," Janet said, taking her mom's hand and securing the insulated tote on her shoulder while her dad picked up the suitcase.

"What about Mr. Happy? I can't leave him here by himself again. Do you mind if he comes along?" she pleaded, trying to mimic Mr. Happy's puppy dog eyes, which did the trick on her parents who both nodded.

"See that, Mr. Happy? You're coming with us. Let's go," she motioned to the hound to walk with them, thinking she really needed to buy a leash for him, though that was low priority right now.

After one last backward glance at her damaged home, Janet joined her parents in walking down the sidewalk toward the cars.

# Chapter 19

Lugging a garbage bag full of ruined clothes from what remained of the guest bedroom closet, Janet trudged outside toward the dumpster parked in the driveway. Mr. Happy, who'd been tripped over multiple times in the clean-up process, lay against the brick exterior by the front door safely watching everyone going in and out.

The insurance adjuster had been by the previous afternoon to assess the damage caused by the storm and had sent a crew to remove the fallen limbs earlier that morning. With the limbs gone and just tarps covering what was left of her roof, Janet had finally been able to start moving things out of the destroyed rooms shortly after lunch.

A contractor was scheduled to come later that afternoon, so Janet's parents and brother-in-law were pitching in to clean out and salvage as much as possible while Julia stayed home with Lucy.

She paused, hands on her hips like an elementary school cheerleader, to rest for a moment after tossing the bag in the dumpster. Her mom came up and tossed another bag in.

"Are you okay, sweetie?" she asked Janet, patting her gently on the shoulder.

"Yeah, my nerves are just shot," Janet answered, raising her eyebrows and widening her eyes as though she were shocked, then relaxing her face and shaking her head low.

Janet had never experienced so many ups and downs within such a short period of time, and each time she felt drained. Within forty-eight hours, her emotions had bounced from bored at home on the couch as the storm began, anxious as the weather worsened, shaken from her encounter with Russ at the nursing home, exhausted from a night on her feet, peaceful when she'd stood in the courtyard looking at the roses, frightened when she saw the news, devastated as she reached her backyard, thankful she hadn't been at home when the worst came through, uncertain about how Marcus would respond when he found out, and now resolutely determined to do what needed to be done without shedding any more tears.

She set the filthy box on the kitchen table, unsure whether or not she even wanted to look inside. The last couple days had been difficult enough without pouring out the old hurts she'd packed away in that box.

Standing by the table, Janet tentatively picked up the soggy cardboard lid and peeked inside. The stuffed white bunny with the big pink bow around its neck, given to Janet by her great-grandmother at Easter when she was nine, was damp from the rain but otherwise unharmed. She took the bunny out and set it on the table.

Underneath the bunny lay the lace handkerchief she'd tucked into her bridal bouquet with the thirty-year-old handwritten poem by her own mother. Blurred from the rainwater, Janet could hardly make out the words:

I'm just a little bonnet
to warm your tiny head,
but with a couple stitches loosed,
a hankie I'll be instead.
And when you find Mr. Right
who lives to make you smile,
I'll be something old
for you to carry down the aisle.

The pain of letting go of the dream of passing down this heirloom to her own daughter hurt Janet tremendously, and it brought tears to her eyes.

"I made that when I was pregnant with you," Sandra said quietly as she walked up from behind Janet to join her in the kitchen.

"I know. I saved it for all these years for nothing." Janet choked back tears. "Why did I even bother? Now it's ruined."

"No, it's not. And you did carry it down the aisle just like I had hoped you would, so it was worth saving." The older woman comforted her daughter. "Life isn't perfect. Crap happens! Even if it was destroyed, it's just a hankie. Your memory of it is the same whether you have it to hold in your hand or not."

Janet sniffled and wiped her nose. "But I wanted to pass it down to my daughter, and I'll never be able to."

"Aw, phooey! I'll sew a new one for my granddaughter if I ever have one! Don't you worry about that!" she assured, giving Janet a pat on the back. "Don't dwell on things you can't change, baby. Focus on what you have, and enjoy it with all your might!"

Janet nodded. "I know. I need a minute to myself though, if that's okay."

"You take all the time you need. I'm going to go check on the guys," she said and left the room.

Clutching the hankie in her hand, Janet walked into the backyard for a few minutes of solitude to get a grip on her emotions, so she could get back to the tasks before her. If the wooden swing hadn't been crushed by the tree, she would have gone over to sit for a while. But she walked over and leaned against the trunk instead, her back against the knot where their initials were carved.

And there she prayed.

"Lord, I'm tired of hurting, I'm tired of being disappointed, and I'm tired of being angry. I can't keep hanging on to things I can't change. You know how badly I've wanted to be a mother, but for whatever reasons, you haven't made it happen, and I'm tired of wishing."

She looked up to the sky through the remaining thick branches and held the hankie out in front of her. "I'm giving it to you, Lord. I'm letting go and letting you handle it. Please help me, give me the ability to move on from this, so we can go on with our lives."

Her eyelids closed, and Janet took several steady deep breaths, her head leaned back resting against the bark.

The spring breeze ruffled the fresh new leaves at the top of the oak tree as Janet rocked gently on the swing below, basking in the miracle of new life and new growth and amazed by the works of God's hands as she surveyed the backyard that had slowly come to life over the last week with color

A grin spread across her face as she watched Marcus complete the final bit of construction at the corner of the yard, meticulously sanding each sharp corner and sinking each nail to make the playhouse as safe as possible.

Since they had finished installing the chair rail and painting the newly refinished guest room a combination of pastel pink and tan the day before, building the playhouse was the only task left before being ready to pick up their two-year-old daughter from the adoption center tomorrow.

Feeling her stares, he turned to Janet. "What do you think?" he asked, spreading his arms open wide toward his handiwork.

Beaming, Janet replied, "She is going to love it! She's going to love *you*." She wiggled her finger toward him and impelled. "Come here." She smiled as she brushed her hair from her face.

Marcus laid his hammer down on his toolbox and walked over to join his wife on the swing. The pair rocked quietly for a while, delighting in the pure joy of being together.

"I can't believe this day is finally here," Janet whispered, laying her head on his shoulder.

"Just think," Marcus breathed deeply, "today is the last day you and I will be here in this house, just the two of us, for a very, very long time."

"I know!" she exclaimed excitedly before cheerfully adding, "Kinda scary, isn't it?"

Janet giggled, happier than she ever could've imagined being.

"God is good," Marcus said.

Janet lovingly gazed at her husband and smiled. "And his plans are perfect."